# Reggie & Me

# Reggie & Me

Marie Yates

Winchester, UK
Washington, USA

First published by Lodestone Books, 2014
Lodestone Books is an imprint of John Hunt Publishing Ltd., Laurel House, Station Approach, Alresford, Hants, SO24 9JH, UK
office1@jhpbooks.net
www.johnhuntpublishing.com

For distributor details and how to order please visit the 'Ordering' section on our website.



ISBN: 978 1 78279 723 4



A CIP catalogue record for this book is available from the British Library.

Design: Stuart Davies

Printed in the USA by Edwards Brothers Malloy

# Acknowledgement

Thank you to my wife, Jill, who has encouraged me every step of the way and to Reggie, who has taught me that every day can bring a new adventure!

'That which does not destroy you,
makes you stronger'

# (July)

It has always been just the two of us. Mum had me when she was nineteen and while she prefers to call me a 'surprise' rather than an 'accident' we can safely say that I wasn't planned. I know that my dad's name is Daniel and that he promised my mum he would stand by us both, love us both and give us everything our hearts desired. Mum was head over heels in love and called me Danielle after this wonderful man. The ink wasn't even dry on my birth certificate when he told Mum he couldn't cope and was leaving to 'find himself'. That was just over fifteen years ago. Daniel is obviously still lost.

I think he's the main reason why Mum has never wanted to move house before. We live in the same house as we did when I was born so he would always know where to find us. She has never been interested in going out with other guys and I love that it is just the two of us. We get on well most of the time. She has her moments and gets unusually upset when I leave crumbs on the kitchen worktop, but other than that, we don't really fall out. Moving away is going to be a really big deal for both of us.

# One

When it first happened, I wanted to run away.

But as time has passed, I am starting to feel settled again and my friends are no longer treading on eggshells. That was one of the worst things for me, seeing my friends struggle to talk to me. They didn't know what to say so they didn't say anything. I didn't know what to say either; I just wanted things to go back to normal. In the space of 24 hours we'd gone from talking about how much we hate maths and what we were going to wear to the party at the weekend to a painful and awkward silence. I was still me. I had just been given a 'victim' label and now that was all people saw.

My mum told me that I did not have to take on the label of 'victim'. She told me that I was strong, that I had survived, and that the most important thing was that we stick together. I didn't really know what she meant at the time. I didn't feel strong, and there were days immediately afterwards when I wished I hadn't survived at all. Mum took the phrase 'sticking together' very literally in the early days. I couldn't even go to the loo without her. I felt like a victim though. The police called me a victim at every stage when they carried out their procedures and the courts weren't much better, either.

At least he pleaded guilty.

Now that the court case is over, he won't be seeing the outside world for a minimum of eight years. It's time for Mum and me to have a new start.

This journal was a present from Mum on the day of the verdict. She said that I need to see my future in these pages. The pages are blank, just like my future; I can create whatever I want on them. The only thing she had written was a small quote on the inside of the front cover, which said, *'That which does not destroy you, makes you stronger.'* She told me that I could look back on it in years to come and see how far I'd come. I think it was her friend Jane's idea to be honest. She's a psychologist and is always coming up with bright ideas to help us both. I dread it when Mum gets off the phone after a couple of hours chatting with Jane. We always have a little task or something to talk about. I must admit that this was one of Jane's better ideas and even though it has been sitting on my bedside table for the last three weeks, I'm actually quite enjoying writing in it now. If only I could have been this enthusiastic at school.

So this is my new start.

I'm writing very neatly as I have only just begun, I give myself about three days before I'm back to a rushed scrawl that Jane will probably think is a coded cry for help and I'll be set another task.

# Two

So, the new school is just like any other school. Big, pictures on the wall and full of kids. The new house looks great; it's brand new and bigger than the one we have now. My room will look out onto the garden and it's much bigger than the box room I've lived in all my life. More importantly though, we're getting a dog! I've always wanted a dog but Mum said that it wouldn't be fair because of us being out all day. Now that we're moving and things are going to be different, Reggie is a new addition to our family.

He's massive but really he's just like a giant teddy. Within seconds of meeting him, he had rolled over and wanted his belly rubbed. Mum was trying to point me in the direction of a smaller dog that she had spotted, but Reggie wouldn't let me leave. He looked at me with his big, sad eyes and I was smitten. I said to Mum that we'd always feel safe with Reggie around and that was it. She agreed that he was going to be ours!

Reggie is two and has had a horrible start to life. He was with another family that sounded similar to us. A mum and daughter who lived on their own. Unfortunately, that's where the similarity ended as they had mistreated him and he had been taken away from them. The horrible child had even attached pegs from a washing line to his ears, which made him bleed and cry. I promised him there and then that he would never be hurt like that again. Mum started crying as she had said the exact same thing to me a few months ago. Bev, the lovely lady from the rescue centre, was almost in tears too, but she wasn't sure why. She had grown attached to Reggie and said to us that he needed to go to a family who knew how to deal with a big dog. At seven stone he is a very big dog, yet as he lay there with his head on my lap he just looked so vulnerable. Mum said that she completely understood and I panicked, thinking that maybe she was going to say 'no', that he'd be better off with someone else. Then she looked to me, then to Reggie and said to Bev that when she had me she had no idea how to look after a baby, but she learnt very quickly. She said that by the time we picked Reggie up in a couple of weeks, she would have read every book on his breed, booked us into dog training classes and bought everything he would ever need to settle in to our family.

Mum then quite innocently asked, 'What is his breed by the way?'

At that point, Bev had stopped filling in the adoption paperwork and I thought Mum had blown it for us. She hadn't even read the description on the door of his kennel. I knew that Mum just wanted to buy the right book because buying books is her answer to everything. It's a shame she doesn't read them all, but I didn't like to mention that. Bev smiled as she said he's a cross breed: half German Shepherd, and half Rottweiler. Mum's face was a picture! Bev quickly added that people quite often get the wrong impression when they hear what he is, and that's why he's still looking for a home. They both looked over to see Reggie gently nuzzling me to play and wagging his enormous tail in utter contentment.

I can see myself in him... He is misunderstood. Because of his breed and what had happened to him, people just make assumptions. I only needed to look into his eyes to see that there wasn't an aggressive bone in his giant body, and that all he really wanted was love and someone to play with. People look at me in the same way. They don't assume I'll be aggressive (I hope!), but they see a child from a single parent family, hear what happened to me and assume things about me. They think they know me.

They don't.

Like Reggie, I can still have fun, still smile (Reggie does smile, really!), and still laugh (okay, Reggie doesn't laugh but he does wag his tail a lot).

I hope that when I start my new school they can see me for

who I really am, not who they *think* I am. I'm nervous about the new school but as nobody will know what happened, I'm hoping that I'll be able to make friends without people worrying what to say or do around me.

I have plenty of time to worry about that though.

First of all, we have to move house, get everything Reggie needs and then go and collect him. I wonder if he's nervous about moving in with us?

I like to think he chose us as much as we chose him.

I think Mum is as excited as I am about Reggie moving in with us. She's made me promise that I'll do my fair share of walks and that I'll feed him, brush him, entertain him and still make sure I do my homework. She made it very clear that we would also be sharing poo bag responsibilities, but I'm not thinking about that. We stopped off at a pet shop on the way home (not that it will be 'home' for much longer), and had to put the back seats down to fit his new bed in the car! At that point Mum asked herself, 'What am I doing?' But I pretended not to hear and was still laughing at the fact she had bought two books. One about German Shepherds, and one about Rottweilers. I did say that she wouldn't be tested, but she was adamant that she wanted to know everything so she could give Reggie what he needed. I spent the rest of the journey home looking at the pictures and getting more and more excited about our new family member.

# Three

'It has been found that spending quality time with a dog can reduce stress and improve your overall health.' That's what the books say anyway. Actually, both books say it so we should get double the stress relief! Mum did not find this funny as she was tearing her hair out trying to de-clutter and pack up the house. I was trying to be helpful, but once I'd packed up my room, it turns out I wasn't much help at all. It's the same when we go shopping. We get to the checkout and no matter how I pack the bags, it's never right. I don't understand why we can't just chuck everything in and then sort it out when we get home. Mum seems to think that there's an order to packing the bags, getting everything in the 'right' order while getting it out of the trolley apparently makes it easier.

Packing up my room was a weird experience.

I found things that I'd completely forgotten about, and it's as if my life is now split into two segments.

'Before' and 'after'.

I found some amazing things from my childhood like photos and drawings. I say that like my childhood is over, which in some ways I suppose it is. I guess that doesn't have to be a bad thing though? It's good that my childhood addiction to painting is over as I don't think I was ever going to have a future in that. I can't believe some of the awful paintings that Mum kept. Although, she did keep them in a box in my room, so maybe she wasn't all that impressed after all. I think I can count on one hand the amount of paintings that made it onto the walls downstairs, and now I understand why. Life was simple back then. The biggest things I had to worry about were doing my homework, what was going on with my friends, and whether Mum would let me have a sleepover. The thing is, when I think about it logically, that's all I have to worry about now too.

Just because it's happened, doesn't mean I have to spend endless days thinking about it. I will have new homework to worry about, new friends (I hope) to consider, and hopefully in time, they'll want to come over for a sleepover. I wonder if Reggie would like a house full of my friends?

I heard a loud bang.

I was about to tell Mum that she really should let me help when I found her in tears, quickly trying to hide all the things that were scattered across the living room floor. I'd never seen the box or the newspaper cuttings, cards and letters that Mum was desperately trying to grab before.

I did not expect to see his face.

Mum was apologising and saying that she'd clear it up and make us both a cuppa (her answer to everything), but I said I'd help. I avoided picking up the cutting with his face on it, but instead picked up a card with a very cute picture of a cat on it. The cat was reaching for a sunflower on a gorgeous sunny day. I opened the card and it was from someone called Sarah. This is what it said:

*Dear Danielle, my name is Sarah; I am sixteen now but two years ago when I was fourteen I was raped too. Like you, I knew the person that did this to me. Unlike you, I didn't have the courage to tell anyone. I want you to know how brave you are and that you have inspired me to tell someone. I said it out loud for the first time yesterday and already things are getting better. I have support and don't feel so alone any more. Thank you... If it wasn't for your bravery I would never have done this. Now I know that I will survive and life will be great again.*

*Thank you from the bottom of my heart, Sarah x*

Mum handed me a pile of cards that all had similar messages. Neither of us moved as I sat and read every single card and letter. They were from people of all ages, men and women. Every single one of these people had been raped, and every single one was writing to share their story and tell me that they were thinking of me. Some people had kept it a secret for years, some had been inspired by my story (like Sarah) to tell someone what had happened to them, and some had reported it immediately, like me.

# Four

I had been sent loads of cards and letters. It was incredibly kind of people to take the time to write to me, I felt like there were just so many of them.

So many people who had been raped.

We're in a small town and because I wasn't in school for a little while afterwards, and I had a lot of support, we didn't worry too much about keeping everything a secret. I could have done if I'd wanted to though.

I asked Mum why she hadn't shown me the cards before. I wasn't angry; I was just a bit confused as they were such kind messages of support. Mum said that she didn't want to put any additional pressure on me, and that Jane thought that maybe it would be too much what with the court case and everything – good old Jane.

I spent all night thinking about what I should do now I'd seen the cards. I felt bad that I hadn't said 'thank you.' A lot of people didn't leave their full names or an address, so I guess that they didn't want a response, which, in a way, was really kind, but I really want to say thank you.

I went through all of the cards again and it wasn't any easier reading them a second time. I collected all of the ones who had names and addresses included, and while Mum was packing up the rest of the house, I wrote a reply to each and every person.

This must be how my friends felt when they found out what had happened to me. I didn't know what to say, but I wanted to say something. I was so grateful that people had taken the time to write to me that in most cases I just said that. I just said 'thank you' and told them how grateful I was. It's always great to get a thank you card, isn't it?

Mum has been pretty quiet since I found the cards.

She said that she has underestimated how strong I am. I'm not sure that's true. It wasn't easy reading all of those cards, but at the same time, it probably wasn't easy for all of those people to write the cards. Nothing about this is easy. Seeing his face on the newspaper cuttings has triggered something in my head. He's been popping up in my thoughts, and last night I had a nightmare about him. That hasn't happened for a while. I used to have nightmares all the time, but since he's been caught and locked away they've started to ease.

I think that moving house and living with Reggie will help.

'Happy' triggers help too.

Little things to make me smile.

This has been a bit challenging now that we're packing up, so right now, I have two. One is a picture of Reggie; I've put it as the screensaver on my phone. This has helped me a lot as Reggie is a sign that things are going to change for the better. I'm scared of all the changes: the new home and the new school. But the excitement about Reggie joining our family is outweighing the fear.

I'm going to look at the picture before I go to sleep tonight. I'd much rather be dreaming of the life I have waiting for me than the life I'm leaving behind. The second happy trigger is a bracelet that Jane gave me before the court case. It's a really nice black leather bracelet with charms on it. At the moment I only have two charms, but two is enough. One is the letter 'B', which she told me stood for the fact that she believes in me 100 per cent. The other is a red glass charm with hearts on it. She bought me this because red is the colour of courage and the hearts are to constantly remind me that I am loved. I thought it was a bit naff at first, but I haven't taken it off since the day she gave it to me. Throughout the court case and the difficult days, it was really comforting. Just having it with me all the time and being able to look at something that reminded me that I wasn't on my own. As much as people told me that they were supporting me, it was sometimes difficult to remember. Especially when you're on your own and feeling scared.

It's only two days until we move house now.

I'm having a final day with my friends tomorrow and I have mixed feelings about it. I want to see them, but it will only make it harder to say goodbye. I thought that leaving them would be the hardest part of moving, but I'm actually looking forward to a clean break.

I know that my friends did their best, and I know that if I were staying here I'd be making much more of an effort to see them, which would make things much better much quicker.

When Mum told me about getting a dog my first thought wasn't to tell my friends, it was whether my new friends would like him and come over to our new house.

I haven't even met these friends yet.

Writing about Reggie is as exciting as talking to someone about him. I'm not sure if that makes me a bit of a loser or just a realist about the changes that are coming. Maybe I've just grown up in a different way because of what's happened.

I see things differently now and understand that there's more to life than worrying about who is talking about you, or who fancies who. Two days to go and I'll be unpacking in my new room. I'll be making a fresh start and preparing for a whole new adventure.

# Five

Today has been full of mixed emotions. I've gone from not wanting to leave at all to being ready to pack the car and never come back. Maybe I was naïve to think it would just be like old times. The day started off okay as we went into town. This is something we have done a million times, but sometimes it just felt fake, like we were all having a day out together because we felt we should, not really because we wanted to. We made the most of the morning though. We'd tried on outfits we couldn't afford and put on ridiculous make up before the shop assistant came over to ask if we needed any help. Her tone of voice didn't exactly make us think she wanted to really help us at all, and we made a very quick exit. In one shop I actually laughed so hard I cried as we were all trying on clothes that our grandmothers would be too embarrassed to wear, and wondered how I would ever cope with moving away and starting again.I wanted a fresh start when it happened; I wanted to escape. But while I was standing in that shop, laughing with my friends, I couldn't imagine my life any other way.

That feeling didn't last long. We decided that we'd go for a pizza and, without the distraction of shops and grumpy assistants, we struggled to find things to talk about. We went through the usual stuff like laughing about things that had happened in school. The only thing was that I didn't remember most of them happening as I wasn't told at the time. Apparently the snotty head boy had been caught around the back of the PE store with a girl from Year Nine, and one of two of the girls in our year, who had been voted most likely to be pregnant before the exams (it was an unofficial vote!), had phoned up to be on Jeremy Kyle. It seems that there were lots of funny things happening while I was desperately wishing my friends would just make an effort to talk normally around me. Although, maybe if I wasn't so busy wishing they'd act normal and just tried to act normally myself, I would have known what was going on and had a great distraction. I don't know if knowing someone who has appeared on Jeremy Kyle should count as a claim to fame, but it would definitely have been a distraction. It took so much effort for me to get to school and get through the day that I almost then expected everyone else to make the rest of the effort on my behalf. 'Normal', what is that anyway?

I thought I'd give it a go while we were waiting for our pizza to arrive and just laughed along with them and asked a couple of questions about what happened. It was just too easy. They told me the stories, we laughed and it felt 'normal'. It felt good. Then as our food arrived and we got stuck in, someone asked if I was looking forward to moving. All eyes turned to me and as I looked up, it hit me that this would probably be the last time that we would all be sitting around eating pizza together without a care in the world. It also hit me that I didn't feel too sad about that. It is time for a change.

I told them about Reggie and how excited I was to finally be getting a dog. They looked at me like I was from another planet. Apparently having to go out for walks and picking up poo is not something that they found all that exciting. Their loss, but I was a bit gutted that they just laughed about it when getting a dog is something I'm really excited about. They didn't even want to see the picture, so I quietly put my phone away and tried to hide behind my pizza as my eyes nearly leaked, it must have been the chili. Their complete lack of interest just showed me that I had changed, and probably grown up a bit, while they were still much more interested in what colour their nails were and how they were going to get the attention of the hot geography teacher. I have bitten my nails since before I can remember – much to the annoyance of Mum who has kept 'stop and grow' in business for the last few years – so I couldn't care less about the colour of nails. I also don't see the attraction with Mr Geography, who makes no attempt to hide the photographs of his very pretty wife, so I don't think he's worried about the attention of the soon to be Year Elevens.

We ate our pizza and split the bill without any more talk of me moving away. They said that they were going to treat me to a trip to the cinema after we had eaten as a goodbye present, but I'd had enough. I didn't tell them that, it was a nice thought, but I said I had promised to help Mum pack.

It wasn't the emotional goodbye I thought it might be.

We all said we'd miss each other and promised to keep in touch, but I knew we wouldn't. I didn't believe their words. Never mind *their* words; I didn't believe my own. I watched them all walk away and they didn't look back.

I didn't feel sad, I felt strong. I was no longer relying on other people to make me feel like I fitted in. I didn't need to fit in. I always thought that 'fitting in' would be the best way to be happy and have a lot a lot of friends. Today proved to me that I could be really happy by following my own ideas and not just laughing along for the sake of it. So what if I want to get up and stupid o'clock and walk a dog in the rain. They would never understand that it's not just about early mornings and poo bags, it's about wanting to feel safe again. As I walked away, I felt a real sense of freedom. I now have the opportunity to be whoever I want to be. I guess that if I was staying around here I would still have that opportunity and would probably just have made more effort to redevelop the friendships, but this completely clean break feels really good. I won't have any history or anything that I need to explain. I can create my own history where I'm not just the girl who's had a rough time. I'm just a girl who is having a fresh start. Now all I need to do is decide exactly who this all new and improved version of me will be.

I think that today has been the first step in finding her as I didn't feel like I had to pretend any more. I didn't stay with them and go to the cinema simply because I felt I 'should' or to make them feel better. I wasn't rude as I certainly don't want that to be their final memory of me, but I also wasn't the timid girl who'd been around for the last few months. I was assertive and it felt good. This has gradually been happening more and more over the last few weeks. I couldn't even decide whether I wanted a cuppa or not when it first happened, but gradually I've been able to make decisions again. I didn't need to make decisions at first. Once I told Mum and we went to the police, everything just kind of happened. At home I was looked after, fed and watered. I didn't need to decide what to eat as Mum did everything for me, I didn't need to decide where to go as I wasn't leaving the house, and I didn't even need to decide what to watch on TV as Mum was checking every programme to make sure there wouldn't be anything that would upset me. Before, I wouldn't have given a trip to the cinema a second thought. If that's where everyone wanted to go then I'd happily have gone along too. Today felt different. I just didn't want to go. Actually saying it, not being rude about it and thanking them for the thought, reminded me that I could take back a bit of control over what I wanted to do and that it was okay to do that.

In the book I'm reading about training dogs it says that you should always remain calm and assertive so that the dog knows who is in charge. Turns out that works on humans too!

# Six

I am sitting in my new bedroom, surrounded by boxes, and rather than unpacking I thought the most productive thing I could do was write in my journal. It could be that I really need to write or it could be that I'm just brilliant at avoiding the jobs I don't want to do. Either way, I'm not going to be doing any unpacking in the near future!

Today was the big move. It started off well with the removal van and a team of guys turning up. Mum was getting slightly neurotic about whether they'd be here on time so she was very reassured when they were a whole four minutes early. They must be used to slightly neurotic people though as they were very patient with Mum as she went through a detailed explanation of how important every single box was.

Mum cried as we locked up our house for the final time. I suppose that if it wasn't for everything that has happened she wouldn't even have thought about moving. I know that a little part of her would be thinking of Daniel too. I couldn't help thinking that maybe this was a good thing for both of us. Mum couldn't spend the rest of her life in this house just on the off chance he might turn up one day. I couldn't care less if he never turned up. I kept that thought to myself though.

As usual, we had packed up a picnic for our journey. The search for the cheese had created a small panic this morning as Mum thought she'd put all the cold stuff in one place and we can't go anywhere without a cheese and pickle sandwich. Luckily the crisps, jaffa cakes and Haribo had been spotted, and I can't say I worried too much when we couldn't find the apples. We had all of our really special things in the car with us. It was a four-hour journey and as usual, we travelled for about 10 minutes, got on the motorway and then started on the sandwiches. I don't think we have ever actually left our picnic alone for more than 20 minutes, regardless of what time of day it is or how far we're going.

We had about an hour to ourselves in the new house before the removal team arrived. Mum had thought of everything though and magically produced two mugs, teabags and milk from a little cool bag. She'd even remembered to pack a teaspoon. We sat on the floor in our brand-new, empty, beige living room, cuppa in hand and continued tucking in to our picnic.

I had remembered everything about our new house and I immediately felt safe. As it is brand new, on a new housing development it really is just ours. Nobody has ever lived here before and that feels really special. It also means that everything is beige and magnolia. That's okay though as Mum said we can put our pictures up and make it our own. There's a rule about not painting the walls for a few months apparently, but there aren't any rules about posters and pictures!

I just sat there, on the floor of my new room. It was a completely empty space. No furniture, no curtains, not even a lampshade. A brand new start.

My special boxes couldn't be unpacked until I had something to unpack them into, so I did what any girl in my situation would do and tweeted a picture of my empty room. Nothing is real until it has been tweeted. It is official, I have moved house and I have no idea what to do next.

The peace was soon shattered with the sound of the removal team bringing everything in and trying to get everything in the right rooms. Mum was explaining once again the importance of each and every box. As she was getting more and more high-pitched I just wanted to apologise, but they took it in their stride. If I had a pound for every time she said, 'Careful, watch the walls,' I'd be a millionaire. Watching them get the sofas in was quite entertaining. In this new house, our living room is on the middle of three floors, so they had to get the sofa up the stairs and around a very tight corner. I was seriously impressed that they managed to do it without making even a tiny mark on the magnolia walls; no doubt it was thanks to Mum telling them to be careful.

The picture I had drawn of my room was coming to life. My desk is by the window so that I have natural light and can make the most of the view into the garden. My bed can only really fit along one other wall as I have brand new fitted wardrobes, and then my little stand for my stereo fits perfectly behind the door.

With the stereo set up and P!NK playing at full volume there was only one option. Dance around the room. This was probably the only time I'd be able to see the carpet so I made the most of it.

All the boxes we had packed up were left in the designated rooms under the watchful eye of Mum who only took a break from her supervisory role to make more tea. I admit that I could have been more useful, but when Mum reaches that level of high pitched-ness (is that a word?!), it's best just to stay out of the way.

My dancing was rudely interrupted by a knock on the door and an unusually smiley mother. Our shopping had been delivered. Seriously! Mum had even done our online shopping in preparation. We found more Jaffa cakes and the fresh milk, made another cuppa and sat looking at the boxes for a little while longer.

So this is me unpacking! I said I'd start on my room. I've been sitting here ever since. My desk only has my journal and pencil case on it, and it is amazing how clearly I can think without all the usual piles of paper, books, magazines and unfinished homework around me. No doubt I'll start off with a tidy desk and a tidy room and within a week it'll look like a bomb has gone off in here.

Here's to my new start. I can get my room to look any way I want it to look, and I can do the same with everything else. I thought I'd feel lonely, but I felt lonelier when I was with my 'friends' yesterday. There is something quite liberating about being anonymous and free to just be 'me'. I am so much more than what happened to me, and now I have a chance to be the person I am meant to be without also having to challenge people's perceptions of me as a victim.

But first...I need to unpack.

# Seven

Waking up in our new house was quite a surreal experience this morning. At first I didn't know where I was and I felt quite scared. Then it all came flooding back. My old life had gone. I thought about calling one of my friends, but I couldn't figure out why. We didn't have much to say when we were together, so I wasn't sure what we'd say on the phone. If in doubt, tweet. I sent them a tweet saying I missed them and immediately had tweets back saying they missed me too. That was enough to cheer me up, it's exactly the same thing I would have done if I was back in the old house, which seems a bit silly now. I can't actually remember the last time I spoke to any of them on the phone. Mum doesn't start work until I start the new school so we have lots of time to get settled in and find our way around. It's not long now until Reggie will join us too. That's currently my only motivation to get the boxes unpacked and everything sorted!

As soon as I thought about getting motivated and doing some unpacking, Mum called me downstairs where I was greeted with a full English breakfast and a cuppa.

Now, I could get used to this.

She said it was to celebrate the start of our first full day in the new house and that I shouldn't expect it every day. I was just thankful her voice had returned to its usual pitch.

How many females does it take to figure out how to use a dishwasher? Two...plus the power of Google as we had lost the instructions. We didn't have one in the old house and it was one of the things we were really looking forward to having here...if only we could figure out how to use it!

There are still quite a few boxes to unpack thanks to my ability to do everything except empty them, so I was quite pleased when Mum asked if I wanted to go and explore the town. She said it would be better for us both than having a quiet day at home. She also pointed out that we may not be able to have days out in the same way we used to when Reggie arrives, so we should make the most of it now. That's true I suppose. Although I still can't wait to go and collect him.

After I was raped, it was the quiet times that I found the hardest. I think Mum still worries about me having too much alone time as sometimes my head can wander back to the dark times. It's not that I need to distract myself all the time or that I feel like I need to be busy in order to cope, it's just that when I spend long periods of time on my own without anything to do I can struggle to focus on good things. When my mind wanders like that I sometimes find myself thinking about what happened and then the old horrible feeling of fear come flooding back. The word 'fear' is used a lot, but that really doesn't even begin to cover it. Complete and utter terror doesn't really explain how it feels either. A part of me just gets deflated, all of a sudden I feel like any control I thought I had has disappeared, and I don't trust myself even to make a simple decision like what to wear or whether to have Hula Hoops or Skips to eat. I guess that sounds a bit ridiculous, always Hula Hoops right?! It just isn't that simple when I slip back into the dark times. I just don't see the point of anything and even though it sounds a bit dramatic, I genuinely don't care if I just stay in bed all day. When I feel like that I don't care that I'm on my own as who would want to be friends with me anyway? It's more than just not caring, it's like the part of my brain that makes me, me, has been punctured like an old bike tyre. No matter how much nice-ness people try to pump into it, there's nothing happening. It's only me who can fix it, stick a magic patch over it and pump it full of my own nice-ness. I love that new word. It can take a while to get myself back from there and it could be so easy just to get under the duvet and not make the effort to do anything. I remember those days though; I spent a fair few days under the duvet. We can safely say that they were not happy days. They weren't supposed to be happy days. As everyone kept telling me, 'It'll take time for you to recover' and 'You need to deal with this in your own way so that you can recover.' Nobody could tell me when I would 'recover' though and what 'recovery' would actually look like. So, for me, recovery is an inner tube! I'll probably keep that one to myself as Jane would no doubt have a few things to say about it.

When I broke my wrist a couple of years ago I remember people making similar comments to me about needing to take time to recover, only they came with timescales and tangible things that I could look out for to tell me that I was recovering. When I had the plaster off I honestly thought I would never be able to move my wrist again. I was scared and it really hurt! Yet, just as the doctor and the physio said, it was better within six months. I did as I was told, did my exercises and now I have a fully functioning wrist again. I do wish the same thing could happen this time. There isn't a programme to follow, a simple tried and tested formula to lead me to recovery, and there's nobody to tell me what it would look like when I got there.

Those duvet days were horrible though. While it does take more effort to get up, get dressed and start the day, it feels a million times better than just lying in bed thinking. It was when I started getting up and dressed again that I realised too much thinking time wasn't good for me! Even the process of deciding what to wear and how to do my hair, helped me to just start thinking about other things again. That's a little rule I have for myself now. Even if I have no plans for the day, I get up, have a shower and get dressed. By the time I'm ready I have often thought of something to do, even if it's just read a book or watch a film. I wouldn't have chosen to do that while I was just lying under the duvet.

So days like today really help me.

A day in town, having lunch out and spending half an hour trying to remember where we'd parked the car are a million times better than the duvet alternative. Before I was raped I would probably have hated the idea of a day out with Mum. It's not that we don't get on; it's just that I would have found 'better' things to do. Now, I am so grateful to be alive and have the chance to enjoy days like this that I try and seize the opportunity. I also can't afford to buy myself lunch out and don't have anyone else to go with, but that's not the point. It feels good to have laughed, to have had some fresh air and to have started our new life here with a good day.

# Eight

I've been here four days now and only have two boxes left to unpack. That's pretty good going for me considering there was a grand total of 17 in my room to start with. I have promised that I'll unpack them today though, as tomorrow is the day that we go and collect Reggie. The agreement was that the house would be completely ready before he arrived. Considering Mum has managed to unpack and sort out the entire house in less time than it has taken me to unpack my room, it's only fair that I stick to my end of the deal.

I got Reggie's little space ready yesterday. I say 'little', his bed takes up more space than mine. He'll be sleeping in the kitchen and that's where we've created his space. We have the new water and food bowls ready which say 'DOG' on them just to avoid any confusion. His giant silver bed has a single duvet in it, and we found a cover that had paw prints on it along with a matching blanket. Mum decided that it would be softer and more comfortable for him than traditional dog beds that also seem to be about four times the price. I tried it out and it is actually very comfy! We've got a toy box for him too as one thing we are not short of is boxes. I have even written 'Reggie's Toys' along the side and added a paw print just to prove that I really do find anything more interesting than unpacking.

I've had a couple of messages and a few tweets from my friends but nothing too inspiring. It seems absence doesn't always make the heart grow fonder! I haven't really thought about them too much. I don't want to make them feel awkward by constantly wanting to be in touch. I don't really have anything new to say to them and I know they won't care it is Reggie-Eve. It's tough when they're talking about starting Year 11 and all the things they have going on. I won't be a part of any of it and I'm not sure I really want to hear about it. The new school has given me some work to do as they were freaking out about the fact my old school used different exam boards. I couldn't get too excited about it as surely Maths is Maths and it's hardly like History will have changed that much! I don't want to turn up on day one without a clue though so I've been keeping myself occupied with the work. I know for a fact that my old friends won't want to talk about catching up on Maths homework and I don't blame them. I also know that if I spend all day tweeting and don't get the work done now there's very little chance that I'll be choosing to do it once Reggie arrives!

I was in top set for almost everything in my old school. I'd quite like that to be the same in the new school. I admit that Maths and French are not my strong subjects; I guess I've only ever done enough to get by, but I do okay in everything else. I have no great desire to go to France, or have a career that involves simultaneous equations, so I'm not too worried. I just have to get a 'C' or above in Maths and I'll get into sixth form. I know that everyone says that there's a lot of pressure in GCSE year and the new school did bang on about how much catching up there would be, but I just don't feel pressure in the same way. I want to do well, I want to go to sixth form and I want to eventually go to Uni, but I just don't get stressed anymore. That might change when I actually start this school year but, right now, I know that if I do the work, do my best and nothing scary happens, I'll be okay. I've certainly gained some perspective if nothing else.

I didn't think I'd be willingly doing schoolwork in the summer holidays, but it's keeping me occupied. As much as I hate the Maths and the History of Medicine is quite disgusting to read about it is keeping my inner tube pumped up. I don't have time to worry about going back to the duvet days when I need to find out how Karl Koller discovered that cocaine could be used as a local anaesthetic in eye surgery. I am almost interested. Mum's been doing some preparation work for her new job too, so we have tried not to get on each other's nerves too much. I like to work with my music on, but Mum needs complete silence. We compromised and I turned my music down and shut my bedroom door, and then while she made lunch, I blasted it out at full volume. We've yet to meet our neighbours, I hope they weren't in. I got quite a lot of work done even if it was mostly cocaine related and feel like I'm getting myself prepared. It's really the only thing within my control.

What is completely out of my control is every other aspect of the new school. I don't know what the other kids will be like, what the teachers will be like or whether the reason I moved here will come back to haunt me. I feel myself getting scared when I think about those things. An ache starts at the bottom of my stomach and rises into my chest; I go cold and then feel my palms getting sweaty. Is that normal? At the moment I'm happily cocooned in my new little life. Just me and Mum in our fab new house looking forward to the arrival of Reggie when our peaceful existence will be shattered! It is scary to think that it's not long until I have to venture out into the real world again. Just the thought of it has made my stomach start aching again. Starting a new school and facing all those people won't be easy. I wonder if I'll fit in. It's been a very long time since I made friends. I went to secondary school with the same group of people I was in primary school with, so it was very easy. I don't really remember making friends with anyone else, it just sort of happened. I should have taken more notice but it was just too easy. We were all in the same position with being annoying year sevens trying to readjust to being the youngest when only a few weeks earlier we'd ruled our school.

This time it will just be me. Everyone else will have their friendship groups and I'll be the new kid without any idea what to do or where to go! Great! For now though, there's no point ruining the rest of my summer holiday worrying about that. I can do without the sweaty palms. It certainly can't be any worse that the first day I walked back in to my old school after everyone had found out about the rape. It looked the same: grey, old and with the usual peeling paintwork. It smelt the same, the usual smell of 'school dinners' coming from the canteen regardless of the time of day and it sounded the same: loud. It just didn't feel the same. I just wanted to shout from the rooftops that I was the same person. I hadn't changed and they didn't have to look away from me. That was when I first noticed I had the ache in my stomach when I was scared. I'd never been nervous about school before, never really been nervous about anything. Was it my imagination that the loud hum of laughing and chatting got quieter as I walked through the gates? Were people looking in my direction and then looking away as I caught their gaze? I honestly think that a couple of the teachers avoided looking me in the eye, which made me feel particularly special! I thought they'd be able to act normally even if the rest of the students couldn't. As if I wasn't nervous enough. However, I also walked through the school gates expecting everyone to treat me differently, so who knows if that actually happened or I just saw what I was looking for. For all I know, the kids were probably just chatting and never usually looked in my direction anyway, and the teachers were just busy being teachers! Being the anonymous new kid will be a breeze!

# Nine

He's here, Reggie is here! As I write, he is sound asleep on the living room floor and it feels like he has always been part of our family. Although, the living room doesn't look quite as big as it did yesterday, and there are already slobber marks on the windows from where he has been checking out the view. Mum is thrilled about the windows. Hmmm!

Even though Mum keeps saying that she's getting the dog for me, blah, blah, blah, she was up earlier than I was and had packed everything we needed to collect Reggie before the rehoming centre had even opened. I saw her reading through the books last night too, just in case we were given some sort of exam.

We were half an hour early to meet Bev, but I think she expected it as she was ready for us and didn't seem to mind. We were welcomed like old friends as I guess she must be used to people like us trying to remain calm whilst actually wanting to just run in and take our new friend home. Mum wouldn't stop talking about everything she had read and how we have everything ready for him. If I wasn't so excited I would have been embarrassed. Bev explained to us that he would be going for his final check over with their vet in the next half an hour. That meant we had half an hour to play with him if we wanted to. That is possibly the most stupid question we have ever been asked! We waited not very patiently, and Reggie came bounding out to us. He looked so handsome and had obviously been brushed in preparation for his big day. He wouldn't stay still long enough for us to stroke him so we opted for ball throwing instead. Turns out I'm not great at throwing the ball very far.

The appointment with the vet went really well despite a small challenge trying to encourage a giant dog onto weighing scales when the last thing he wanted to do was sit. Reggie was signed off with a clean bill of health. That was a relief! He couldn't get out of there fast enough and certainly wasn't as emotional as Bev about the fact he was leaving. She cried as we took him to the car and Reggie didn't even look back. He jumped in the boot without us even having to ask, and panted all the way home. I couldn't stop looking at him and had to keep telling Mum to look at the road! She just kept staring at him through the rear view mirror.

When we got home he dribbled water all over the kitchen floor, had a quick bite to eat and knocked Mum's entire collection of cook books off the cabinet in the kitchen with one swoosh of his giant tail. We tried to get him to lie on his bed like Bev had shown us. He did it perfectly at the rehoming centre, but that was obviously just a ploy to get us to believe he was well behaved! He lay on his bed for all of three seconds and then went off exploring the house.

He didn't get far as Mum had closed all the doors to the rooms he wouldn't be allowed in, which was most of them! He was as excited as we were, I think. Mum gave me the full lecture about starting the way we wanted to go on with Reggie, and that he needed to know who was boss. Apparently, that's her and not me! She used her best 'mum voice' and demanded that Reggie sat down and then lay down on his bed. I don't know who was more surprised...Reggie, that he wasn't top dog or Mum, that her command had worked. Either way, Reggie was on his bed and looking at Mum for his next instruction. He was thrilled that the next command involved sitting down for his lead to be put back on and he definitely understood the word 'walkies'!

Taking Reggie out on his first family walk was an experience. We decided not to let him off the lead until we had spent more time at home practising his recall. After the drama we'd had in the kitchen we weren't convinced he'd remember his name, let alone come back to us when we called it! Bev told us that he pulled on the lead a bit so advised us to get a Halti – it's something that goes around his muzzle (nose!) to help stop him pulling. With seven stone of powerful dog, it's amazing how much that little Halti helps. We walked for about two hours and Reggie was amazing. He stayed close to us, was obedient when we needed to cross the roads, and even gently approached another dog to say 'hello'! We won't dwell on the obvious down side involving the shared responsibility of the poo bags, but Mum is sticking to her guns on that one.

I have literally never been happier.

We are now all exhausted as the excitement of the day is turning into tiredness. Mum and I are half watching a film, but can't stop looking at Reggie sprawled out on the living room floor surrounded by toys and treats, like he owns the place. He is gorgeous. Every few minutes he wakes up and looks at one of us as if he's just checking we're still here. The slightest move we make means he looks up to see what's happening. I hope he'll settle and realise that he's here for good. I hope he will feel as safe with us as we feel with him! It's not that I consciously don't feel safe here, but I will go to bed tonight feeling more secure than I have in a long time.

# Ten

I can't believe Reggie has been here a week already! The time is flying by and I have done absolutely no schoolwork and haven't written in my journal either. I've been having too much fun! Although I did learn the hard way that not everything about having a dog is fun. On the first night he was here, I went to bed feeling on top of the world. What could be safer than a home with a giant dog? Well…I was sound asleep, so was Mum. Reggie was in the kitchen. Nothing on earth could have prepared me for the fear I felt when he started barking at 3.46am. I was literally frozen in my bed. Surely no dog would make that amount of noise for nothing and I was convinced that there must have been someone in the house. I couldn't even make myself get out of bed to check if Mum was okay. While I was trying to talk myself into a more rational state, Mum rushed into my room apologising. She had rolled over in bed and her book had fallen on the floor, waking Reggie. I cannot even begin to describe how loud that bark was and how ferocious he sounded. It took at least another half an hour for my heart rate to return to normal.

Other than that little setback, living with Reggie is brilliant. I have never been more motivated to get up in the morning. Mum and I are still taking him together and he's getting really good at coming back when we call him. There have been a couple of scary moments when something much more interesting has diverted his attention, and he has sped off in the opposite direction. One was a squirrel, which we understood, but the other turned out to be a plastic bag blowing in the wind! He has made friends with other dogs, which meant Mum and I have been meeting people too. It's weird to think that I hadn't actually talked to anyone except Mum since we moved here! We have become part of a little dog walking community, which is strangely friendly. Some dog walkers have been a little unsure when Reggie has been running at full speed towards them, but thankfully he's always stopped just before he has been close enough to knock anyone over! He is really gentle with other dogs and that has made life a lot easier as we are trying to be accepted!

Getting to know Reggie is a real learning curve and it's obvious that he's had a rough start in life. We were all in the kitchen yesterday and Mum stretched her arm over Reggie to reach into the cupboard above where he was sitting. He flinched as if he thought she was going to hit him. I immediately went to stroke him but Mum stopped me, saying that the book said we mustn't reward him when he does that as he'll think it is okay. He needs to learn that he's safe and that he will never be hurt by us. That was really difficult for me as all I wanted to do was comfort him! I felt so angry that someone could have done that to Reggie. I knew a little bit about the things that had happened to him but I wasn't prepared for seeing how it still affected him. I guess I naïvely thought that now he was in a happy home he'd forget all about what happened. Stupid hey?! I'm in a happy home and I haven't forgotten what happened to me either.

I think Mum read my mind as she handed me a cuppa and said that she will never forget how she felt when I told her that I had been raped. Her eyes welled up as she said that it's a mother's worst nightmare that someone would hurt her child. She had never said that me before, and whilst I obviously know that it had a profound impact on her, I didn't realise the anger she must have felt on top of everything she was feeling for me. She said that she is grateful every day that I told her and even admitted that she felt proud of herself as a mum that she had raised me in such a way that meant I could go to her. Yet she would never forget the intensity of feelings that she experienced when I told her what had happened. I had absolutely no idea how she must have felt. I didn't cross my mind for a second that I couldn't go to her about what had happened to me. I literally ran to her. When Reggie cowered, I had a small insight into how she must have felt. It's instinctive. I just wanted to protect him and make everything better. Mum wanted to do that for me too and yet nobody can.

Just like with Reggie. We can't take away what has happened to him, but we can do everything in our power to make sure he is looked after, make sure he is happy and that he knows he is safe with us. As I looked at Reggie, his tail was wagging and he was clearly over his moment of feeling frightened! I needed to take a lesson from him in getting over my scared moments. He just seems to be able to do it so quickly whereas I'd spend half the day trying to talk myself around. It's just tough when I am feeling pretty good and then something happens to burst the bubble. That happens instantly but doesn't work so well the other way around. I still have my bracelet on and have plenty of things to keep me positive; I just need to work on speeding up the process.

There have been a lot of lessons for all of us in this week. It's been strange, but going for walks with Mum has meant that we have talked a lot more. Not always about deep and meaningful stuff, but just talked about things we'd like to do now we're somewhere new and memories of fun times together. I have learnt some embarrassing stories about my childhood too! Apparently when I was a toddler I used to cry to get out of my buggy and then run as fast as I could before crying 'bloody murder', to quote Mum, and refusing to be put back in. I sound like I was a fabulous child to be around. More than anything, there has been a lot of laughing. Mainly at Reggie rather than my childhood escapades! He has really brought us closer. I have even started to master the 'mum voice' that makes him do as he's told!

# Eleven

I'm so glad today is nearly over as it means Mum will calm down again. It was the first time my grandparents (her parents!) had come to see us in the new house. We don't really see much of them so whenever they come and see us it's a really big deal. Mum spends at least two days fretting about it and cleaning everything in sight. It's not that they're horrible people (most of the time); we're just not that close.

During the court case they said some things to Mum that caused some tension. Apparently Mum wasn't looking after me properly and not keeping me safe. She was distraught when they said that as she was afraid that's what people would think. She also did feel responsible even though there was absolutely no reason why she should. I had walked that way home from school every day for a couple of years! How she could possibly feel responsible was beyond me. Hearing someone say it out loud really hurt her. Especially when it was said by the very people she needed for support. Needless to say, we didn't see a lot of them after that.

Today was the first time we'd seen them since the court case had ended and, thankfully, everything had calmed down. We were on safe ground in our new home and Mum was trying to build bridges. We had told them that we'd got a dog now, but they hadn't really asked anything about him on the phone. Reggie welcomed the knock on the door with his usual deafening bark, which meant they were a little quiet when we opened the door. Reggie was still in the kitchen because we weren't completely sure how he would react. After all, these were our first visitors in the new house.

Mum said that she'd leave the guided tour until later and sent them to the living room with me while she made tea. They gave me a big hug and asked me how I was doing. They used 'that' voice though. The voice that is softened and always accompanied with a tilt of the head and a gentle nod. When I said I was doing great, loving the new house and excited about them meeting Reggie, they continued to nod with concerned faces. Then they said, 'It's okay, you don't have to pretend with us, we know how hard it is for you.' Great. Firstly, no they don't know. Secondly, I was telling them the truth. I could sit in a corner weeping and wailing if that would make them feel better, but it certainly wouldn't make me feel better. Before I had a chance to respond, Mum had arrived with the tea. She could see by my face that they had obviously already started, so returned to the safe conversation options of how their journey was and what the weather had been like. We didn't really care about either, but at least nobody could get too upset by the traffic building up on the motorway, and the weather forecast for the day that may or may not include drizzle.

I asked them if they wanted to meet Reggie as I was desperate to introduce him and also pretty intrigued to see how he'd react to new people being in his house. They still didn't ask anything about him, so I just went downstairs, opened the kitchen door, and he bounded up the stairs with all the decorum of a baby elephant. He made it up to the living room much faster than me and by the time I got there it was clear that my grandparents were not impressed. Reggie had his head in Grandma's handbag and had whipped Grandpa's knee with his unstoppable wagging tail. Mum finally got him to lie down but he was very excited and wouldn't stay down for long. He came and sat with me and was happily showing off his new trick of offering me his paw. Even this did not impress them as they were slowly regaining some composure, and Grandma was wiping slobber from her handbag.

'What the hell are you doing with a dog like that? Hasn't Danielle been through enough?' my Grandpa said. Our balloon of excitement had been burst and utterly deflated.

I could see that Mum was utterly disappointed and frustrated.

All she wanted to do was show them that she was doing her best for me. She really is an amazing mum, yet they just want to criticise her at every opportunity. Before she had a chance to speak I said, 'Just look at him. Don't look at the black and tan Rottweiler face or the giant German Shepherd tail. Don't see his muscle or his oversized teeth and don't judge him based on what you think you know. Just look at him. He's lying here next to me offering me his paw. He is gentle, loyal and all he really wants is for someone to rub his belly!' As if on cue he rolled over and with all four legs in the air he lay there as I stroked him. 'How scary is that?'

Mum smiled at me with a tear in her eye as both of my grandparents came over to stroke Reggie. He was basking in the glory of all that attention, and Grandma just looked at me and said, 'You're right, he's not so scary after all and maybe you really are doing okay.' It seems it wasn't just Reggie she had taken the time to look at. She had looked at me too.

That was all it took for us to actually have a really nice day together. They were complimentary about our new house and even treated us to a delicious lunch. We took them on walkies this afternoon and it turns out that Grandpa is a pretty impressive ball thrower. I'm sure that they were sorrier to leave Reggie than us this evening. Can't blame them!

# Twelve

Shopping is never something I really want to do, but when it involves school uniforms and a whole list of other things I'll need for the upcoming educational adventure it's even less fun than usual. We tried to make it slightly more enjoyable with a pub lunch but even that wasn't really helping. It was becoming real now. I guess that moving away and getting Reggie had been so exciting that I'd almost forgotten that the summer holidays wouldn't last forever. My safe little cocoon was about to unravel. I'm not completely sure I'm ready for that to happen yet.

Trying on the new school uniform upset me more than I thought it would. It suddenly hit me that I may never see my old friends again, and I actually had quite a nice life before. With the obvious exception of what happened to me, I was happy there. My friends hadn't deliberately upset me; they just had no idea how to deal with such a difficult situation. I know that they did the best they could. Nobody had ever talked to us about rape and it certainly wasn't a topic of conversation at school. It was weird but I remember someone talking about what had happened to me and then talking about sex education in the same sentence. One of the more dopey teachers had asked me if I was doing okay being back at school. I went with the easy option of 'yes, thanks', as I didn't really have a clue whether I was 'doing okay' or not. She asked if there was anything she could do and then asked if there was anything the school could have done differently 'like better sex education' or more information about 'how to protect myself'. Like that would have helped?! Unless they were going to issue everyone with a security guard to walk them home I'm not sure how 'more information' would have helped and as for better sex education. What the hell did she think had happened to me? Did she think it my fault or something I wanted? Silly cow. I often wondered if people would have reacted in the same way if I had been beaten to a pulp and had very obvious physical scars. By the time I returned to school, the bruises I had were long gone and I looked exactly the same as I did when I had last been there.

Talking about sex was always a bit of a laugh and a joke, but obviously, what happened to me was no laughing matter. Jane had spent hours with me explaining that what happened to me was violence and that sex had been used as a weapon. I just was never sure how to put it into words and I wish I'd been braver about talking to my friends. After my 'chat' with Mrs Dopey I wanted to tell my friends about it, but I just didn't know how. They asked if I was okay as they noticed I'd stayed behind after class. I couldn't find the words and before I had a chance to answer I heard one of them say, 'So is anyone else wearing blue to the party this weekend as I don't want to clash.'

A fierce look was shot in her direction followed by, 'Like Dani wants to hear about your stupid colour issues, there are bigger things happening in the world you know.'

I wish I could have found the words to explain to them that they can still talk to me in the same way they always had. I wasn't wearing blue because I hadn't been invited and nobody had even thought to mention the party to me. Just because someone had been violent towards me in the most horrific way, I hadn't lost the ability to be a friend. I wanted to be there for them as much as I wanted them to be there for me. I wanted to talk about colour clashes, why I thought her latest boyfriend had stopped texting her, and what was going on at the weekend. I know that they had their own stuff going on, but they just didn't want to burden me with what they considered to be little things. As I stood there in my new uniform, feeling alone, frightened and a little bit silly, I just burst into tears.

Mum sensed some apprehension and paid for the uniform in order to get us out of there quickly. Unfortunately our speedy exit has resulted in a slightly oversized regulation pullover and a polo shirt that would be tight on Barbie. That aside, I just felt completely overwhelmed.

I wanted to call my old friends, but, at the same time, I never wanted to see them again. I wanted to start school and get that first day over with, but, at the same time, I never wanted that day to come. I wanted to explain to Mum exactly what was going on in my head but I had absolutely no idea where to start.

What came out of my mouth was a hysterical mash up of random words, which even I couldn't make sense of. Mum didn't stand a chance. She picked up all of the shopping, put her spare arm around me and guided me back to the car. I felt so stupid! I was doing really well, but all of a sudden my little head went into overdrive. Back at home, Mum put the kettle on to make a cuppa and I took Reggie up to the living room.

Just sitting with him calmed me down. With a cuppa in hand, I just said to Mum that I felt completely overwhelmed. 'Mum, it all feels too much, I don't know what to do.'

'Do you want to talk about it, love?' Mum asked, but I couldn't. Sensing my lack of words, she left the room for a moment. On her return, she bought back some felt tip pens and paper.

'If you can't say it, maybe you could just write it or draw it?'

So I did. I ended up with a giant spider diagram of what was going on in my head. No wonder I was a mess. It took me ages and as soon as I wrote one thing down, twenty more things would pop into my head. There were things popping up that I didn't even realise I was thinking about. Mum just sat quietly on the sofa, not saying anything and not reading what I was writing down. Reggie lay next to me, occasionally looking up, and resisted the urge to eat the pens.

I felt exhausted when I'd finished. Exhausted and very relived. Just getting it out of my head without anyone interrupting or feeling like I had to talk was brilliant. I love having this journal but just having a giant, blank piece of paper that I could brain dump onto was very therapeutic.

'Sorry, Mum.' I wanted to apologise for my outburst in the uniform shop.

She just laughed and said, 'It's amazing the lengths you'll go to, to get out of uniform shopping.' She told me that she has sometimes done this with a giant piece of paper too and that she feels a bit scared about starting the new job! It was nice to know that what I was feeling was completely normal! It turns out that grown-ups aren't all that sorted either. I think I'll sleep well tonight as for the first time in ages my head doesn't feel like it's spinning. There's a lot to be said for a decent brain dump!

# Thirteen

Only two days until I start school. The fear keeps coming and going. Ever since my mini breakdown in the uniform shop I've been feeling a lot calmer. I decided that I'd write to my friends so that at least I had said some of the things I wanted to say.

Hey,
I'm about to start the new school and it has made me think about you. I just wanted to write and say thank you for all those years of friendship. I have so many happy memories, like when we thought it would be funny to burn an incense stick in the English lesson and the new teacher lost it trying to figure out where the smell was coming from. Dropping the bag of sweets that we shouldn't have been eating in the French class was another highlight and not embarrassing at all! We've had a lot of fun and I am really going to miss you. I hope you don't miss me too much as you start the dreaded Year 11. Good luck. You know I'm just a phone call away if you want to catch up and if you ever want to come and stay it would be great to see you.

Miss you,
Dani x

It was a relief once I'd posted them really; I didn't want to constantly be wondering if I could have done more and at least this way I've hopefully made them smile.

One of the other things that I didn't realise I'd been worrying about was leaving Reggie. Apart from a few trips into town, Mum and I hadn't really left him on his own. We've started to get him into a routine this week and I'm feeling a bit better about it now. It turns out that once he's had his long morning walk and his breakfast he'll happily just go to sleep! He wakes up when the post is delivered and lets the world know he's here, but otherwise he is sound asleep. When Mum starts work it's going to be my job to walk him. I've been taking him by myself and he's perfectly well behaved. I also feel really safe when I'm out with him. All of these things had been playing on my mind and once I'd written them down I knew that I could do something about it. Mum had been worried about me going walkies on my own too, so it's easing her worries that I'm enjoying it so much. The big park near where we live thankfully has street lights all around it, so even when it starts to get dark it will be okay. Mum had thought about all of these things when we moved. All I thought about was how to arrange my room!

On our walk this morning I let Reggie off the lead as usual and he went running towards his favourite tree. He saw a squirrel there a couple of weeks ago and now has to check every morning if the squirrel is back. I saw a guy walking along the path towards me. He was dressed in a suit, carrying a briefcase and talking on his mobile phone, so there was no logical reason why I felt my blood run cold. I was really scared. As he walked towards me, I don't think he even noticed I was there. I felt Reggie's cold, wet nose touch my hand and he stood beside me. He must have sensed that I was frightened as usually he was far too busy on squirrel patrol even to glance in my direction. Reggie sat next to me, staring at the guy on the phone. He had certainly noticed I was there now and looked at me as if to ask if Reggie was friendly. I smiled at him and said, 'He's fine.' The man smiled back and carried on walking. There wasn't anything to fear for either of us, and a simple smile was all it took for us both to be reassured. I felt safe and so grateful that Reggie had behaved like that. He certainly looks like a dog you wouldn't want to mess with, even though I am not completely sure what he would actually do if I needed protection.

The selfless act of abandoning squirrel patrol was worth it for Reggie as Mum was so proud that she cooked him chicken for dinner. She even called my grandparents to tell them about it.

I have spent this evening getting everything ready for school. Like all the other things I've worried about, when I actually do something about it I'm not quite as frightened. I have my uniform ready and I hope that it will be a warm day so that I don't need to wear my oversized pullover. All of my stationery is packed away and I have the real essentials ready in my new bag: lip balm and tissues. I'll be taking my own lunch as both of my experiences of school dinners weren't great. According to the woman we spoke to earlier this year, I'd be getting everything else I need at the start of term. I even walked Reggie to the school gate this morning to work out exactly how long it would take. About six minutes! Mum had thought that through too as she didn't want me walking a long way to school any more. One annoying thing is that the jewellery policy says I can't wear my bracelet. I'm getting into a habit of taking it off in the morning and putting it back on in the evening, so I don't miss it too much. It's amazing how attached I've become to it. As a replacement to make me smile, Jane sent me some red pens and pencils that would comply with school rules and still remind me to be courageous. They're packed! So, there's not much more I can do to prepare. The scary is part is not knowing what's actually going to happen.

I wonder if anyone in my new Form Group even knows that they'll be a new kid starting? I wonder if they'll even care? We called it Tutor Groups in my last school. I hadn't ever considered what it must be like for a new kid starting school. We had a couple of new kids throughout my time in my old school and I didn't give it a second thought. Now, I wish I'd made more effort to at least smile at them.

# Fourteen

The best part of today was the Chinese takeaway we've just eaten.

I made it through my first day, but I'm not really feeling the love for going back tomorrow. I guess it could have been worse, although I'm not sure how.

I got there on time despite Reggie choosing this morning to roll in something that doesn't even bear thinking about. I had to hose him down when I got home, so I was running late and worried that it was a sign of how the rest of my day was going to go. I was right. Washing Reggie was actually a highlight! So, I turn up at school in time to hear the first bell and find my way to my Form Group as I was instructed. The teacher, Miss Haywood, spotted me and welcomed me in. 'You must be Danielle.'

In that moment, the room went quiet and the rest of the class just stared at me. So much for remaining anonymous. I found a seat without much trouble and listened as Miss Haywood explained to us that Year 11 was the most important year of our lives and it would make or break what we wanted to do in the future. Feeling suitably uninspired I was given my timetable. As if the day hadn't already started badly enough I read that I would have to endure Maths every Monday morning for the next year. This had to be some sort of cosmic joke. All of a sudden I had Grandpa's voice in my head saying, 'Hasn't she been through enough?!' I smiled as I caught the eye of a fellow Form Grouper. She didn't smile back.

Miss Haywood pointed me in the right direction for my first lesson and said that she would be in that room all day if I needed anything. I wasn't sure I'd ever find it again but thanked her and headed off by myself in the direction I'd been sent. To be fair, the lessons weren't too bad. We were getting the same lecture in most of them to start with. This is the most important year of your life, concentrate, work hard, blah, blah, blah. At least I could just sit and listen so I was quite grateful that I wasn't expected to interact with anyone. As the day went on it was becoming clearer that I would have a lot to catch up on and that things were quite different here. Whilst I was right that history hadn't changed, I wasn't expecting it to repeat itself. I was about to start work on 'Medicine Through Time' for the second year running! I had studied this last year and again in the summer holiday thinking that I would never have to do it again, I needed to catch up on Modern World History by myself. That should keep me out of trouble and help me sleep!

Break and lunch times were the worst. I just sat by myself. I could see everyone else catching up on the gossip and laughing about what had happened in the holidays. I desperately wanted a group that I could go and talk to, but at the same time, the thought of having to talk to anyone scared me. They would ask where I was from and why I left. Mum and I had agreed that if anyone asked, we would say that we moved for her job. That was nice and easy but I still didn't want to talk to anyone about it. I wasn't sure why I felt so scared though. Was it normal to feel like this or was I scared that people would find out about what happened?

They were the longest breaks of my life.

At the sound of that final bell it was like I'd been freed from prison. I almost ran home, got changed in record time and was out with Reggie before I could give school a second thought. At least he was pleased to see me. It was so nice to have something else to focus on as otherwise I think I would have moped around feeling sorry for myself. Instead, I was in the park watching Reggie playing with a dog half his size. There is no better distraction!

It was Mum's first day at work too and she came home armed with the Chinese takeaway. This was a very pleasant surprise. She had sent me a couple of texts during the day to see how I was getting on and I just replied saying I was fine as I didn't want her to worry. Especially after she'd admitted she was nervous about starting her new job too.

We sat together, devouring the food and talking about how our days had been. We both said that they'd been good and came up with a couple of stories. The most interesting thing I could think of to tell her was that I'd have Maths on a Monday morning. It then went quiet and we both laughed as Mum said to me, 'Was your day pretty crap too then?'

I was so relieved it wasn't just me and grinned as I replied, 'Yep, it has been a long, lonely day and I'm very happy to be home.'

Mum packed away the empty takeaway boxes and admitted that she hadn't really spoken to anyone either as she'd been handed folders of policies and procedures to read. I don't really know what they are but it sounds about as exciting as having to repeat 'Medicine Through Time'!

As I came upstairs to get some homework done she said, 'It will get better you know, we both just need to give it some time.' That would be easier said than done when I couldn't even get someone to smile back at me, but I kept that thought to myself. She was still sure that moving here was a good thing for us and that it would just take time to settle in properly. I really hope she's right as I'm not sure how many days like this I can take!

# Fifteen

I wish I could say that day two was better.

It wasn't.

Well, in some ways it was as Reggie didn't roll in anything disgusting this morning and I didn't have Maths. Nobody can say that I'm a complete pessimist. School wasn't any better though. Miss Haywood cornered me this morning with an upbeat, 'Hi, Danielle, how are you getting on, are you all ready for day two?'

I didn't really know what to say. I feel like I've got an entire year's worth of work that I need to teach myself, nobody will even glance in my direction let alone speak to me and I'm scared that people will find out the real reason why I moved school. Other than that, I am fine and dandy! So, I stuck with the standard response of, 'Fine thanks, I'm okay,' and she seemed happy with that.

I thought about what Mum said about being patient and making an effort to be friendly. Patience is easy as I don't have an option, but I can try being friendly. I had already endured another day of break and lunch times on my own and it's really not much fun at all. I felt like people were staring at me, but every time I looked up nobody was looking my way. At lunchtime I was sitting near a group of girls who I know are in my year as two of them are in my Form Group. I overheard them talking about trying out for the sports teams for that year. They said that the sign-up sheets were going to be outside the PE block early next week. I kept listening while they were talking and it seems that the school has a successful collection of sports teams. They were listing loads of schools that they were going beat and apparently every other school in the area is crap. It took me back to sitting with my friends at my old school. We were on most of the sports teams and did okay throughout the year. It didn't seem to matter whether we won or lost, the other school was always crap for one reason or another. It's amazing how you can moan about your own school, but as soon as you're on that sports team it's every other school that's crap. Listening to those girls made me miss that feeling of being part of something. I didn't really miss my friends so much, although it would be nice to have people to talk to; I just really missed being a part of something. Maybe I could have that again if I tried out for the teams? It's been a while since I played any sports but I haven't forgotten the rules, and surely if I was on the teams in my old school I couldn't be that bad at it. All I need to do now is find out where the sign-up sheets are when they go up next week. I was tempted to ask one of the girls who is in my Form Group, but I just couldn't bring myself to do it.

What's happened to me? I really didn't think I'd ever be too frightened to go and speak to someone. I felt like I was literally glued to my seat and despite knowing that the simplest thing to do would be to get up and ask, I just could not do it. That's not me. I used to be the sort of person who was first to speak up in class, first to sign up for anything and nobody would ever have described me as shy. I didn't think twice about speaking to other people in my old school whether I was friends with them or not. Now, I'm just scared. Scared of anything and everything to varying degrees. My stomach ache had reappeared at the thought of speaking to those girls and my legs felt too heavy to move. I hate this new me.

After I was raped, I eventually went back to school. I was nervous but I didn't feel as afraid as I do now. My legs felt like they were a normal weight and I had the ability to move them for a start. When we moved house I was more excited than anything, but as the time got closer to starting school I seemed to get more and more afraid. My biggest fear is that people will find out about what happened to me. I didn't really think anything of it in my last school as everything happened so quickly. I guess nothing bad happened as a result of people knowing, but now that it's completely my choice I want to keep it a secret. What would people think of me if they knew? At least my old friends already knew the real me before it happened. People here would surely only see me as a victim. That's the last thing I want as being ignored has got to be better than being pitied.

I couldn't wait to hear that final bell and once again I was home in record time. When I stepped inside the front door, I was greeted with an envelope with some familiar handwriting on it.

Hey Dani,
Of course we miss you! It's not the same here without you but we hope you're having a brilliant time at your new school. We reckon you've got loads of cool new friends and have forgotten about us already because you're having too much fun. It's got to be better than here. We keep getting lectures about working hard for our exams (like we hadn't figured that out) so we trying your trick of putting your head in your hand to look like you're concentrating whilst actually closing your eyes and having a nap! No more sweets in French classes as you need to make a good impression, which won't be hard for you. We'd love to come up and visit when you're free if your new friends won't mind us taking you away from them.

We miss you loads,
All of us x

I cried. I'd been thinking about them ever since I'd overheard that lunchtime conversation and whilst I thought I didn't miss them...I really did. I miss how it used to be though. I miss the way it was before I was raped. I miss how easy it was just to be together, talking about anything and everything. We used to talk non-stop and I can't remember what we talked about! I didn't seem to matter.

More than anything, I miss how I used to be. I used to be someone that people wanted to be around.

At least Reggie enjoys my company! He was thrilled to see me when I came home. Knowing that I have to get myself motivated to take him out for a walk after a bad day really keeps me going. As I'm writing this he is lying across my homework and I'm not feeling motivated to move him. I'm not sure that I can use that as an excuse for not doing it though. He does make me laugh! When I'm with him it's impossible to feel sorry for myself. It's also impossible to get anything done!

# Sixteen

Got to love the weekends! It is just so nice to have time at home again. The summer holiday already feels like a lifetime ago. Mum and I went out for a pub lunch yesterday and it was such a nice way to spend a Saturday afternoon. I didn't say this to Mum but it was just so nice to have someone to talk to! Mum commented that it had been weird not hearing our phones go off all the time. When we were in our old house it was non-stop beeping. Since we moved the beeping has got progressively less! Mum said that she hadn't really heard from her friends either. Her best friend, Jane, was always there for her and the morning beep from her daily text message was still a constant feature in our days. They were always in contact. Jane was in contact with me too, which was nice, but I do wish I had my own 'Jane'! Mum and Jane grew up together and according to my grandparents were inseparable. Then, Jane went off to Uni and Mum stayed at home, but they never lost their friendship. I never really had one best friend. There was a group of us who spent lots of time together but I also floated amongst other friendship groups! I was part of the sports teams and enjoyed singing so also had friends in that group. My main group of friends were great but there wasn't one person I would say was my best friend. Not like Mum and Jane.

Mum said that we'll know when we've settled here because the beeping will start again. I hoped that would happen soon. The only thing I'd been using my phone for is playing games in lunch breaks when I would rather have been talking to people.

'I'm thinking about trying out for the sports teams if you don't mind. If I get selected it might mean some after school practice, so Reggie wouldn't get a walk until a bit later.'

Mum was really pleased and ironically decided to celebrate this decision by ordering us a pudding! She said, 'That sounds like a brilliant idea, you used to love all that team stuff and I'm sure Reggie will cope for an extra hour or so. Does this mean you're feeling a bit happier about school?' I said that we'd need to wait and see. I didn't want to lie and tell her that things were getting better but I also didn't want to worry her.

It was a gorgeous day so it would have been rude not to get home and take Reggie on an adventure. It's not like we had any exciting social plans! We set off to a local park that Mum had been told about by someone at work. At least she had found someone to talk to!

The park was brilliant as it had a little lake that Reggie could swim in. It was the first time we had seen him in water and it was very entertaining. He didn't seem to understand that coming out onto the grassy area and shaking all seven stone of waterlogged pooch wasn't going to win us any friends though. He did completely drench a small child and Mum told me off for laughing! The parent wasn't impressed and the kid wouldn't stop crying. Mum told Reggie off too, but he clearly had no idea what he'd done wrong as he did exactly the same thing again two minutes later! In an attempt to prevent any more small children getting soaked we headed into the dry part of the park!

I was still laughing when we were greeted by a very cute Labrador. Reggie was ecstatic that he'd found a friend and they proceeded to chase each other around the park. We were really pleased as this was by far the best way to tire him out! We found out that the Labrador was called Bailey when his owner came running up apologising that he was chasing Reggie. We very quickly explained that this was not a problem and it was really nice for Reggie to play! Bailey's owner seemed relieved that she wasn't the only one with a naughty pooch as we told her about Reggie's water related incidents. She introduced herself as Jenny and said that she had a daughter, Katie.

We introduced ourselves and Mum launched into the prepared speech. 'We're new to the area as I was offered a job up here that was too good to pass up so poor Danielle has had to move schools too. We're living on the new development near the school, which is nice, but very quiet compared to what we were used to.' She was flawless. I nodded along and smiled in the right places as it turned out that I went to the same school as her daughter and we were in the same year.

Jenny seemed really nice and said she wished her daughter would join her on walks with Bailey. Mum was in full flow and they were talking for ages while I wandered off and entertained myself with the dogs. Reggie was in his element and it was so nice to see him playing. I looked over at Mum talking so easily to Jenny that I couldn't help feeling a bit jealous.

On the way home, Mum said that it was really nice to just talk to someone about normal things. She said that Jenny and Katie also lived on their own and she had a similar background with Katie's Dad. I didn't understand how Mum could just talk so easily about something so personal! The fear started to rise and Mum must have known what I was thinking. She assured me that would never tell anyone what had happened without my permission. The speed with which the fear rose in me really took me by surprise, but I knew that Mum would never say anything. Maybe it was just nice that there are other people out there in a similar situation to us! There's hope yet that we can make friends and build a life here. I could see that meeting Jenny had really given Mum a boost. It has to be my turn next! For now though, it's back to reality and time to get ready for school tomorrow.

# Seventeen

Today did not go quite as well as I had hoped.

When I talked to Mum about decided to sign up for the sports teams trials I had a real hope that it would be the start of something positive for me. In my old school I was on all of the teams and, looking back, I think I took it for granted. I didn't just love the sport, I loved being around people and having a good time in the process. We did have a lot of fun and even though I did quite a lot of moaning about training in the cold or the rain, we always found something to laugh about. I was the reason for a lot of the laughter in hockey as I was very good at sprinting and then falling over as I went for the ball, I would quite often manage to find the muddiest part of the field to do this in, and end up looking like I'd had some sort of weird mud massage just without the posh spa. While I was walking to the sports building I couldn't help smiling to myself thinking that maybe this would be the turning point.

That optimism was short lived! The guys were on one side of the room fighting to get their names on the sign-up sheet and making more noise than necessary just to write their names on a piece of paper. It was as if this was the test in itself. The first people to get their names on the board would be picked! If it was that simple I'd have got here earlier! Looking over to the other side of the room I could see a gaggle of girls doing much the same thing.

I wandered towards the back of the gaggle and waited. I couldn't see the point in trying to push my way to the front and hoped that eventually they would start to move away. I knew that I had to sign up before the end of the lunch break so if the bell went for class I could just come back later. I couldn't help thinking that maybe I'd missed something though. What was the gaggle about and why the desperate urge to sign up?

As I hung back I could hear what they were saying. They were talking about the PE teachers. I haven't met any of the PE teachers but apparently,

'Miss King is all right.'

'Mr Bray is a perv.'

'Mr Jacks is gorgeous.'

'Miss Jones is a lezzer.'

GREAT!

It's not that I'm a huge fan of teachers, but I do know what it is like to be talked about. It just made me a bit uncomfortable, so maybe I am growing up after all. I certainly can't take the moral high ground and say that I've never talked about a teacher. We were always hearing gossip about teachers in my old school, in fact with the names changed I'm sure we had the exact same conversations. It just sounded different today. Unnecessary and cruel.

I think that I was talked about a lot at school. I don't know for sure but I am almost certain that if this had happened to someone else, I would have been talking about it. I still wonder about what people would have said, but I try not to dwell on it or it drives me insane. I think that I would have felt sorry for the person it had happened to. I would like to think that I would have been concerned about them, but I'm not sure I would have known what to say. Yet, when I think of other people feeling sorry for me it makes me uncomfortable. Especially when those people don't know me and don't really know what happened or how I feel. I do, however, wish that more people had just talked to me. Not about what happened or anything like that but just talked normally to me like they did before. I wish that would happen now too though! I'm being ignored here for different reasons but it's a similar feeling of isolation and it's no fun at all.

Hearing what the gaggle of girls were saying about the teachers made me wonder if I really did want to get back into doing things at school. I don't want to be the person that talks about people I don't know. I don't want to make anyone feel the way that I felt.

There was a level of aggression in their voices when they talked about Mr Bray and Miss Jones. It was horrible to hear. From what they were saying, it turns out the Miss Jones is the hockey coach and they were making jokes about the people who'd signed up for the hockey trials. As far as the gaggle were concerned, they all just wanted to spend time with Miss Jones or vice-versa. I'm writing the polite version here too! They were talking about the people who had signed up already and listing other girls who they thought would sign up. I think they even added a couple of names for their own entertainment. On the plus side, I hoped that meant none of these girls wanted to play hockey!

I actually considered not signing up. I was ready to walk away and had come up with all the reasons (excuses!) I needed. These included needing to concentrate on catching up on work, passing my exams, walking Reggie and even time to spend with friends! The irony! It did hit me at that moment that without signing up I am reducing my chances of making any friends, so I changed my mind back again. I waited as the gaggle started to move away from the board and I signed up for the hockey trials. They didn't even notice I was there which was a blessing as they also didn't comment on the fact I'd signed up for hockey!

# Eighteen

I am in the hockey trials.

I know that it's not much to be excited about as I'm sure that everyone on that list has been accepted for the trials, but I'm still excited that there's something to break up the monotony of school. I'm doing okay, getting my work done and not getting any hassle, but there has to be more to school life than this. I know that there is more to school life than this; I just need to figure out how to get it.

I took Reggie out into the garden for some hockey practice last night. He was no help at all as he kept running off with the ball and trying to bite the stick! It kept Mum and me entertained though and Mum even grabbed my old stick and tried to tackle me. Apparently she was quite a good player when she was at school, hmmm…I'm not so sure! Still, I feel like I can at least remember how to hit the ball; I just know that I'm nowhere near as fit as I used to be. With Reggie's help I'll be amazing at tackling by next week. Keeping the ball away from his mouth is great training.

I had to go back to the dreaded board to find out if I'd been picked for the trials or not. The gaggle of girls were there again, but this time they were much quieter. They're not quite so brave in sharing their opinions when they are surrounded by all the hockey players that they were happily badmouthing the other day! That made me smile, I was really intimidated by them before and now I'm not sure what I was scared of. There were so many people there all checking whether or not they had been given a spot in the trials for their chosen sport. Everyone just wanted to see if their name was on that board.

There was one strange moment. I heard my name mentioned and my blood ran cold. I thought that someone was talking about me and I strained my ears to hear more. It was only someone asking who I was! There were a couple of girls at the front looking at the hockey list and they didn't recognise my name. All they said was,

Random girl A: 'Who's Dani Moore, I don't know anyone called Dani Moore?'

Random girl B: 'No idea... Maybe she's one of the new girls that started this year?

Random girl A: 'Oh yeah, could be. I wonder if she's any good!

That was it. I suppose I could have just gone up to them and said 'hi' and told them I was Dani. That would probably have been easier than panicking and straining to listen. It was a positive and pain free mention of my name. What a relief.

Trials aren't until next week so I have some more time to practise the basic skills in the garden. It's not ideal training ground, but it's better than nothing. Reggie had better tackling skills than Mum, but I won't mention that to her! When I think about the trials I feel quite scared; my stomach starts its gymnastics routine, but I'm not completely sure what I'm scared of. I have a cycle of questions going around my head: What if I don't make the team? What if I do make the team? What if I'm rubbish at hockey here? What if I fall flat on my face? I have a feeling that if I do fall flat on my face the girls here won't find it quite as funny as my old friends did. What if the gaggle of girls are all trying out for hockey despite what they said? There are so many things that scare me about this. It's just hockey! When I try and be logical I know that it's just a game of hockey. I have all the kit I need, I know the rules, have played lots of times before and more often than not, I enjoyed it. I have to tell myself that approximately 500 times a day.

I've certainly survived worse than a game of hockey so really, there's nothing to worry about. Really, there's not. If only I could be this logical all of the time. I seem to have days where I feel invincible and then days where I just feel terrified. I am stronger than I thought though. If someone had told me a couple of years ago that I'd be here now, having experienced the rape, the court case, moving house and moving school, and all I was worried about was a game of hockey, it wouldn't have made any sense at all! What's the worst that can happen? Ha ha… My friends and I used to jokingly ask each other that question a lot. They stopped asking me after I was raped. But what's the worst that can happen now? If I don't make the team then at least I know I tried. If I do make the team it'll be a chance to make some friends. I know that I'm not rubbish at hockey; I just have to play to the best of my ability and show them what I can do. So what if I fall over, at least I'll be putting in 100 per cent effort. If the gaggle of girls are in the trials too then it will just be funny as they won't have any idea that I heard what they were saying. There. All I need to do now is remember the logical answers to the questions going around my head.

There's a lot to do before the dreaded trials though…I shouldn't call them that really as that's not helping! There's a lot to do before THE TRIALS! That's better! Top of the list is the homework that I've been avoiding while writing this!

# Nineteen

I feel totally ashamed of myself and that's a pretty horrible feeling. I know that I could have acted differently too, I know that I could have made a difference, but I just didn't have the courage to do something about it. I know that I'm better than that. I know that I'm not a coward. That's why I feel so ashamed.

I had PE for the first time today. I wasn't really looking forward to it but it wasn't as bad as I thought it might be. It was Miss King taking the class and it turns out that the gaggle of girls were right about her; she's all right! She asked me to stay behind after the lesson as she needed to go through some things with me. I have a lot to catch up on to make sure I'm ready for the exams, and she told me that she's been put in charge of making sure I get whatever I need. She even asked if I'd mind being late for my lunch break and if we could go through it now. How nice is that?! I didn't tell her that this would be the first time I'd spent a lunch break with someone.

We went through the coursework I needed to do and she had copies of everything I needed. She also offered to go through the work with me in lunch breaks if I was struggling. It all seemed quite self-explanatory but I really appreciated the offer as sometimes when I look at the volume of work I have to get through it can be quite overwhelming.

'How are you getting on, how are you finding the school?' was the question I was waiting for and she didn't disappoint.

I hope I didn't disappoint with the standard answer. 'I'm getting used to it, thanks, and slowly finding out where everything is.'

I wasn't expecting what came next as usually the standard answer is enough to end this conversation. She smiled and said, 'I moved schools in the year before my exams too. It was tough. Everyone had their own little groups of friends and I just found myself wandering around feeling like a spare part. I had loads of work to catch up on and to make it even more interesting, they were learning completely different things in most of the subjects. I did okay though, just kept my head down and looked forward to sixth form where life became a lot more fun. Hang in there.'

I could have cried as it was the first time someone had actually got how I was feeling. I mean, really got it. She didn't expect me to say anything either which was a bonus as I am not sure I could have stopped talking if I'd started. I knew that I was feeling quite low about the way things were going (or not going!) at school but it wasn't until Miss King spoke to me that I realised what I'm feeling is probably perfectly normal! That half an hour really made my day and I left that room feeling the best I had felt since starting at school.

Then...boom! Just as the cloud had lifted it came back darker than ever. I heard some voices as I walked out of the room but didn't think anything of it. It was lunchtime so it's usually pretty loud and I had never been in the PE building at lunchtime before. As I was about to turn left into the corridor that leads to the main doors I realised that the voices were shouting. I had a quick look around the corner and saw a group of five girls all crowded around another girl. I didn't recognise any of them but I don't really recognise many people yet.

This is why I am feeling so ashamed of myself: I hid. I sneaked into the toilets and I hid. The old me would have marched up to that group of girls and tried to help. At least, I'd like to think that's what I would have done. Today, I was a coward and all I could think about was the fear that it might happen to me. I was too scared to say anything or do anything; I was even too scared to walk past them.

I hid as I heard those girls say some really horrible things. They were shouting in her face calling her all the names under the sun. I'm not even sure what some of the words meant, but I knew I wouldn't want them shouted in my face. I was standing in the toilet feeling like a total failure. I felt so sorry for the girl who was on the receiving end of their verbal battering, but just couldn't summon up the strength to do anything about it. I was as bad as they were.

I heard them shout a final mouthful and then the door slammed. I opened the toilet door and could see that the girl was sitting on the floor crying. I didn't know what to do. I ran back to the room that Miss King was in, she was still there and looked surprised to see me. I said to her that someone was upset in the corridor and I wasn't sure what to do. She took over, found the girl and led her back to the classroom thanking me for telling her. She thanked me? That was the final blow. She wouldn't have thanked me if she'd known. I should have got her straight away as I didn't have the guts to step in myself. I should have gone straight to her and asked for help.

I haven't been able to concentrate all afternoon because I've been thinking about that girl. I need to concentrate this evening though as I have so much work to do. I do feel a bit better now that I've written it down...I just need to get braver as I don't want to feel like this again!

# Twenty

Jane is coming down for the weekend so I am under strict instructions to tidy up. I think that's what Mum thinks I'm doing now! I'm tidying up the thoughts in my head if that counts?!

We have had quite a positive morning so far, although it was a little embarrassing too. We agreed that we would need to make sure Reggie was as tired as possible as Jane isn't a big fan of dogs. She doesn't dislike them but she prefers them when they're asleep or in another room! We set off bright and early and headed to the park with the water. We figured that it was a bit early for small children to be out and about so hoped that Reggie could have some fun without creating a drama. That went according to plan and he was swimming around, playing with the ball and being surprisingly well behaved.

Out of nowhere, he was joined by another dog and was so excited he actually squealed! That's not a sound that fits with the image of our big dog! Mum turned around to check that there were humans accompanying Reggie's new friend and almost squealed herself when she realised it was someone she recognised. It's amazing what loneliness does to you! It was Jenny, the woman we had met last time we were at the park, which meant that it was Bailey who was currently trying to chase Reggie across the lake. Neither of them even glanced in our direction as we called them, so we just agreed that they'd surely come back when they were tired.

I recognised Jenny's daughter, Katie, immediately. She was in my registration group. I'd never spoken to her but that's not surprising considering I hadn't really spoken to anyone. We were introduced and had no option but to talk to each other while our mums were in full flow talking about everything under the sun and our dogs were swimming in circles around a lake. It was awkward to start with. We didn't really know what to say to each other so we started on the easiest subject – school. As we didn't have any classes together other than registration that wasn't a very successful start. I didn't know most of the people she was talking about and she said she was into Art and Music, while I was doing PE. She didn't seem very impressed that I used to sing at my old school! She said that she hated PE and walking the dog was more than enough exercise for her. That led us onto a much more successful conversation about the dogs!

It was so nice to talk to someone about Reggie. I haven't really had the chance to do that and I enjoyed talking to someone else who loved dogs. There are things that only other dog owners would find funny and these are things that you probably wouldn't talk about with anyone else. She told me about Bailey accidently weeing up a man's leg when he was standing waiting for the bus. That was the most embarrassing thing he'd done. Reggie hadn't been quite that bad yet, but I told her about him soaking the child last time we were here. They had had Bailey from when he was a puppy so he's had a great life with them. She was genuinely upset when I told her about Reggie's past, but could see for herself that he was perfectly happy now. She asked how long we'd had Reggie and that led her to ask why we moved here.

It was easy to go with the rehearsed story, and the more I say it out loud, the more comfortable I am with it. I almost believe it myself! She said that it must be pretty crap starting at school and not knowing anyone. She had been at that school from the start and said that while it isn't her favourite place on earth, she wouldn't want to start again somewhere new. 'You'll be okay though, the sporty kids are always popular,' she said. 'It's the arty people like me who never quite fit in and get the comments and digs. I couldn't care less though, only a few more months to go and it'll be time for some sixth form fun.' I didn't mention the girl I saw in the corridor but asked her if she had ever been bullied. She said, 'Not really, I just stick to my own group of friends. I wasn't sure what 'not really' meant but thought I'd better not ask. Then she said that if I wanted to join her and her friends for lunch on Monday they'd be in the main hall and she'd look out for me. She gave me her number and said to text if I couldn't find them. I just said, 'Thanks, that would be nice,' but inside I was squealing! Yes! Someone to have lunch with!

At that moment Reggie and Bailey came running up to our mums and completely drenched them by shaking right next to them! Thankfully we stayed dry but it meant it was time to leave. Mum and Jenny swapped numbers too and apart from the soaking, it has been a very successful morning. Both Mum and I are excited by the idea of new friends. It's amazing how quickly my mood has changed over the last couple of days. From the happiness of Miss King's kind words, to the shame of not helping that girl, and now to excitement that I might actually have made a friend!

# Twenty-One

A day with Jane is always good for the soul, though now I've come upstairs to bed and left her downstairs with Mum and a bottle of wine! It might get a bit emotional and messy so I'd rather be up here.

Jane arrived in style with an enormous bone for Reggie. I thought that she was just being really kind as she knew how much Reggie meant to us. No! Mum pointed out that she had probably just bought the biggest one available so that it would keep Reggie occupied! That backfired a bit though as Reggie went straight out into the garden and buried his treat. He returned a couple of minutes later covered in soil and still smelling a little bit of lake water despite the bath we gave him when we got home from our walk. Reggie wanted to say a big thank you to Jane but she wasn't so keen. He has spent the rest of the day asleep though so our plan did work and Jane is grateful that we tired him out!

Jane brought gifts for us too. As always they were really thoughtful presents. Wellies for walking and a gorgeous photo frame for our first family picture with Reggie! She had come prepared with her camera and we had some fun trying to get Reggie to look in the direction of the camera and sit still all at the same time. I can't wait to get those pictures!

After the obligatory pot of tea and chat about her journey here she asked if I'd like to take her into town and show her the sights. That is a pretty rubbish code for saying that we're now going to go and talk about whether I'm okay or not! I don't know why they don't just say what they mean!

Talking with Jane is always really helpful, but I'm also aware that she's Mum's best friend. I don't want Mum to worry about me so I am a little bit guarded about what I tell her. I wanted to tell her how crap I felt about school, but at the same time I was pretty sure she'd tell Mum. Knowing Mum, I wouldn't be surprised if she came into school to talk to the teachers. I know that she'd only be doing it to try and help me, but it's not like the teachers can force people to be friends with me! That would be the most embarrassing thing that could happen at the moment. I am so grateful that I can tell Jane about my morning with Katie and that I'm pleased I have someone that I can have lunch with now. Jane picked up on the 'now' very quickly and asked what I'd been doing so far. I think I got away with talking very quickly about how I'd been accepted for hockey trials and she didn't ask about lunch again!

Jane thinks that with the amount of work I've got to do and the pressure of making friends I need to be careful about making sure I'm still looking after myself. 'You know that recovery can take a long time, Danielle, so don't underestimate the impact it can have.' She does annoy me sometimes when she says things like that! I'm more than aware of the impact it has had and I'm sure that any professional would tell me that recovery takes a long time, blah blah blah! Maybe I'm doing okay and an acknowledgement that I'm not crying in a corner at every opportunity would be nice. Then I remembered how I felt when I hid in the toilet. I told Jane about it. I made sure that I included the bit about how nice Miss King was!

I could see that she was worried about me and said all the things I expected her to say. 'You did exactly the right thing by going to Miss King. Don't be ashamed of that, I don't know anyone in their right mind that would take on a group of teenage girls anymore.'

I told her that I thought the 'old me' would have tried to stop them and she didn't agree! 'It's easy to think you'll always do the most heroic thing until you're actually faced with that situation. Your perception of fear might have changed a bit now though.' She's not wrong! I am definitely more cautious, but we both agreed that there's nothing wrong with that!

She asked if I was worried about the hockey trials! I swear that woman is a white witch sometimes! I admitted that I was nervous, but I also told her about how I'd thought it through and when I was feeling rational I knew that it was just a game of hockey! She laughed and said that she had taught me well! It's true…she has! She couldn't leave it there though.

'Just relax a little bit, Danielle. You're worrying too much about how long it's taking for you to settle in and you're not giving yourself a chance to just settle in your own time. You met Katie without any effort at all and I bet it didn't feel like effort at all?' Argh, why is that woman always right?

It's true, I've been stressing out about making friends and then a potential friend just arrived at the side of the lake! It was surprisingly easy.

She wasn't finished. 'People are much more likely to want to be friends with someone who is relaxed and easy to talk to rather than someone who is stressed out and worried!' I was definitely relaxed this morning and I had to admit that once again, Jane was right! She makes it sound so easy.

I always feel better when I've spent time with Jane. I would love to be able to help people like she does. She (nearly) always knows the right thing to say and I wish I was more like her. I would love for someone to say this about me one day – that they feel better after they've spent time with me!

# Twenty-Two

For the first time since I started at this school I didn't have lunch by myself! The lunch break I spent with Miss King doesn't count. I didn't text Katie, but as I walked into the main hall she spotted me and waved. That was a relief as part of me was wondering if she was just being polite when we met the other day and maybe she didn't want to invite me to lunch after all! All those fears went away as I walked to the table and started eating my packed lunch. I was introduced to Maya and Callie who had obviously been warned that I might be joining them, and to be fair, they were very nice to me.

In an otherwise pretty dull day, this was definitely the highlight. I don't have any lessons with any of them so there wasn't much to talk about when it came to school. They are all into Art and Music too but didn't seem to mind that I was more into PE. Callie said that she was studying Art so that one day she could be a famous tattoo artist, which I think is very cool. She showed me some of her designs and they were amazing. Katie said that Callie had drawn a picture of Bailey for one of her art projects and it's now hanging on the wall over Bailey's bed. I said that she could borrow Reggie for an art project anytime she likes! She was happy with just a photo and said she'd love to draw him. I hope that she will as I'd love a picture of him up in the house. For the first time, the lunch break was over really quickly. It usually feels like it's dragging on and on forever. It flew by today and I actually feel like I could be a part of something. They all seem nice, although Maya didn't say much!

Geography was a real downer as the group I was in all started talking about the field trip they went on last year. That was a pretty easy way to make sure I was excluded from all the conversations! From what they were saying it sounded like it would have been a lot of fun! I missed the field trip that I was supposed to go on last year. It was at the same time the court case was going on and whilst the police said I could go, Mum wasn't too happy about it. I had mixed feelings as I really wanted to go and just be 'normal' again but I also knew that I probably wouldn't feel 'normal' once I was there! I was a bit nervous about being away from home too. I hadn't been anywhere really since it happened so it probably would have been good for me, but we all decided that I'd stay at home. I was relieved once the decision had been made, but looking back I think I may have been taking the easy option.

Sitting in the geography class with all that going around my head meant that I was just sat in the group looking a bit spaced out. I didn't realise that I was so deep in my own thoughts until I heard the teacher saying, 'Danielle, what do you think?'

Urmmmmm...I had no idea what I was supposed to think as I had absolutely no idea what we were doing! I sat there like an idiot and just said, 'Sorry, I'm not sure.'

'You really need to concentrate if you want to catch up and be ready for the exams.'

Talk about pointing out the obvious. I can't help it sometimes when my mind wanders and I have no idea how to snap out of it by myself. I'm okay when I'm occupied but sometimes when my mind goes back to all the stuff that went on I just zone out. Maybe if I tried concentrating on the lesson I wouldn't zone out as easily! I'll try that! I still have no idea what I was supposed to be doing in geography, but I enjoyed it at my old school and I'm pretty sure the continents haven't moved in the last few weeks, so I should be okay!

By the time I got home I was still feeling pretty good. Thinking about lunch cheered me up and the downer of geography went away. I've got into my routine now, so no matter what has happened at school I know that everything will be okay once I'm home. I get in, get changed, get Reggie and get out! I don't know what I'd do if we didn't have Reggie. I would probably just come home and go over and over the day at school in my head. That's what I'd been doing before we moved and it was really getting me down. Since we moved and I've had my routine with Reggie I have something to look forward to, and getting outside seems to really cheer me up. I feel like I have more energy when I get home and I'm even ready to do some homework. Mum has said she's noticed a difference in me too. I wonder if I'll still feel this positive about walking Reggie when it's cold and raining in winter?! At least I know I'll always feel safe with him by side.

# Twenty-Three

Hockey trials day.

I was ready and as prepared as I could have been. Mum even made me a special breakfast and packed a lunch full of energy boosting food. She had read about it somewhere and so as a result, I ended up with a jam sandwich, a fruit pot and a boiled egg.

I had my kit ready and actually felt quite good as I was getting changed. I'd eaten a bit of my lunch and it did give me a boost to know that Mum had made an effort because she knew it was trials day. Nobody even glanced in my direction as we were all getting changed, but I am used to that now and don't think much of it. Miss King and Miss Jones were going to be watching the game and then picking the team. During the briefing they said that we'd be doing some drills and then playing a game. Instead of the usual 35 minutes for each half we'd only be playing for 20 minutes each half, with a five minute break when they might change our positions. That sounded okay to me!

I got involved with the first set of drills and it felt so good to be playing again. I know it wasn't a game, and I didn't even have anyone to really chat with, but I just felt happy to be moving and out in the fresh air. I looked around and I was certainly keeping up with everyone, I wasn't doing anything silly, and so far I hadn't fallen over.

Then we were put into teams for the game. I hadn't even thought about that, and for a horrible moment I thought I would actually be picked last. That has got to be the worst nightmare of anyone who is doing PE. I had never even considered it before now. It used to be me or one of my friends picking the teams and all of a sudden I felt very, very scared. I breathed a sigh of relief as Miss Jones started reading out names and positions! They had already picked the teams and told us which position we would be playing. I usually played in an attacking role but they had put me in midfield. That's okay though as I thought I'd get a decent chance to show what I could do. Nope!

It was beyond embarrassing. I was tripped up, nobody ever passed me the ball and they made it pretty obvious that I wasn't welcome. I tried to tackle a few times and once a member of my own team shoved me out the way! I didn't stand a chance. I thought I might get an opportunity to play a different position in the second half, but no. I couldn't even stay in the same position! I was taken off to let a couple of other girls join the game. That was it. My 20 minutes of glory had been turned in to the most humiliating 20 minutes since I started here. I felt shattered. I know I can play, I know that I could be on that team and play well. What happened wasn't fair and the ref (Miss Jones) didn't blow the whistle once when she must have seen that I was being shoved.

Miss King came over as I was standing watching the second half and helpfully said, 'Sorry it wasn't easy but they've been playing together for four years.'

So why have the trials then? Why give me false hope that I might actually be able to join something?

'You can go and get changed if you want to, it's getting cold.'

I almost sprinted back to the changing rooms as I wanted to be showered, changed and out of there before they all came back. The shower hid my tears as I just felt so stupid. I still do. I really thought that this was my opportunity to make some friends and start building a life for myself. Instead, I was no longer an anonymous new kid; I was someone who wasn't welcome and someone who needed to learn her place. I've got the message loud and clear. I've got a graze from when I was tripped up to remind me. That made me cry more as standing in a shower with the sting of hot water hitting damaged skin brought back memories too. It was only the thought of them all coming back to find me crying in the shower that gave me the strength to move.

I got changed faster than I ever thought possible and just made it out before they all came back.

I sat by myself, out of sight, eating the rest of my energy filled packed lunch and feeling very sorry for myself. It took every bit of strength I had to hold back the tears, but when I checked my phone and saw texts from Mum and Jane I couldn't hold them in any more. They said that they knew I'd do brilliantly and they were really proud of me. I couldn't think of anything to say in reply so just put my phone away and headed to the toilets to try and get some cold water to sort my face out. I couldn't go into class looking like that. I'd think of something to tell them. I'll just say that this school has a lot more hockey players and that I tried but I didn't make it.

I managed to stay occupied for the last two lessons and even walked past the gym building on my way out of school. I waited until it was quiet and checked the board. I don't know why I bothered as needless to say, I didn't make the team. I wasn't surprised but I'm still gutted. Mum will be home soon so I need to sort myself out enough to be able to tell her something.

# Twenty-Four

Last night was pretty awkward. I had practised what I was going to say to Mum about there being loads of hockey players and I practised my best 'not bothered' face. She was excited when she came home, laden down with my favourite dinner that she was going to cook for me. Chicken Kiev and chips may not sound that exciting, but it is one of my all-time favourites! It's also one of the few things Mum can cook!

As I walked down the stairs I started delivering my speech. 'Thanks for the texts and for lunch, it really helped. I did okay but there are loads of good hockey players and they've all been on the team together for years. I'm not really bothered because I've got loads of work to catch up on anyway.' Then I burst into tears. Complete fail! So much for practising what I was going to say.

Mum came over to hug me saying, 'I know you would have done your best, Danielle, that's never in question. I'm sorry that you didn't make the team but I'm really proud of you for trying. I didn't realise it meant so much to you.'

That made me cry more. I really need to stop with the crying! She thought I was crying because I didn't make the team and I thought it would be easier for her to carry on thinking that. I didn't want to tell her that I felt completely humiliated and the whole thing was a total embarrassment. I just explained that I wanted it to be a bit of a fresh start and the chance to make some friends. She understood that and decided that dinner and a walk with Reggie would be the best way to cheer me up. She was right! Reggie was very excited to be having a second evening walk and I must admit that dinner was delicious. I had a text from Jane yesterday evening too after Mum had obviously passed on the news. 'Who cares about hockey anyway? Can you name one famous hockey player? Exactly!' That was it and she has a point!

It made me laugh until Mum could name two or three hockey players but she soon shut up when she saw my face!

Another horrible day at school has been ticked off along the road to sixth form and I'm trying to get some homework done. I'm obviously not trying very hard as I'm writing this but I need to write to help clear my head. I was absolutely dreading going to school today as I desperately didn't want to see the hockey girls. Thankfully I didn't have PE today so at least I could stay well away from the PE building. I'd happily never set foot in there ever again but sadly that's not an option. I was looking over my shoulder all day and I'm not even sure what I'm scared of. They got what they wanted and I'm not on the team so they've probably forgotten about me already.

It's been a while since I've felt this scared and it's absolutely exhausting. I used to be terrified of the slightest thing, the slightest noise in the weeks after the rape. It was completely irrational as I knew he was locked up but it didn't stop the fear. There was one night when Mum and I were watching TV and she told me that it was probably time for me to go to bed as we had an early start in the morning. I went out into the hallway and none of the lights were on. I could not go up the stairs and even when I turned on the lights I couldn't make myself go up the stairs. I was completely frozen in fear. I still have absolutely no idea what I was frightened of. Mum came out to find me just standing there, shaking, looking up the stairs, and I think at that moment she was more frightened than I was. She held it together though and eventually I went to bed and got to sleep but only with Mum by my side. Thankfully I haven't felt like that since, but today was the closest I've come to feeling so scared over something so irrational. What's the worst that can happen? They say something to me or they push me? That's not nice but it's not the worst thing in the world. I just can't shake the feeling of fear and it's doing my head in.

In lessons I felt safe enough but walking to and from different classrooms was a complete mission. I was on guard the whole way and convinced I would bump into those girls. What was I going to do if I saw them? At break time I spent the whole time in the loo, and while I felt pretty safe I also felt like a complete idiot. It stank too! I really wanted to go and find Katie, Maya and Callie at lunchtime but couldn't bring myself to walk into the main hall. While I'm in this mood I'm pretty rubbish company anyway, so they're probably better off without me annoying them. I ate my lunch by myself and it really feels like I'm back to square one, except it's worse than that as I'm no longer just the new kid. I'm the kid who can't make friends and can't get on the teams. I never thought I'd be 'that' kid!

# Twenty-Five

I've turned in to a total recluse. I need to do something about it or I'll be back to a stage where I don't want to get out from under the duvet. It's been a long time since I've felt like that and at the time I thought it was justified. I don't think it's justified now. I remember Jane saying to me a few months ago that there comes a point when you have to take responsibility for your own future. I thought about it at the time and knew that she was right. Whatever happens in my life, it's only me who has control over how I deal with it.

What I didn't realise was that I'd have to make that decision time and time again. It's not like you can wave a magic wand and say, 'Today I am taking responsibility' then everything is okay. I really wish it was that easy. Almost every day I needed to say that; sometimes it works and sometimes it doesn't. All that mattered was that I got into the habit of trying to take responsibility for the way I reacted to things every day. I feel like I have to make that decision every minute of every day at the moment. It's not just the stuff that happens to you that you need to respond positively to. It's also the stuff that's going on in your head!

I'm not doing a very good job of it at the moment. I have been hiding away, avoiding everything and everyone. I'm not sure I've even spoken to anyone other than Mum in the last two weeks and that's pretty sad. Apart from answering 'yes' to registers and the occasional chat if I've been forced into group work in class I haven't actually spoken to anyone. I had a text from Katie asking where I'd been and if I wanted to join them for lunch. They must think I'm really rude as I haven't seen them since that one lunch break. I wouldn't want to be friends with someone like me right now.

Mum told me this evening that's she's worried about how

quiet I've been around the house recently. I said that I was just stressed about the amount of work I had to do, that at some point soon I'd need to start thinking about sixth form and just that I was tired. She said that she'd take Reggie in the mornings if I wanted to get some extra sleep but I really didn't want her to do that. For a start, it would mean her getting up even earlier than she does already as she has to be at work for eight. It would also take away the one thing that gets me out of bed in the morning. She asked if she could help with any of my homework, but unless she wanted to start writing essays for me there's not much she can do. I know that she's only trying her best but it really is only me who can sort this out.

It's like I'm letting the whole hockey experience stop me from making any friends at all. Seeing that girl getting bullied hasn't helped either I don't think. Why should those girls stop me having friends? To be fair, they haven't stopped me. It's only me stopping me and that's just stupid. They've made it perfectly clear that they don't want to include me in their world, but it doesn't mean that nobody wants to include me. I've made it impossible for anyone to include me in anything. It's not like some random person is going to come knocking on the toilet door begging me to be their friend! If they did, I think it would be okay to be frightened of that!

Looking back over the last few weeks things have started to get even worse since I shut myself away. I started to feel isolated and lonely because I isolated myself. That seems pretty silly when you think about it. The best thing that happened at school was having lunch with Katie, Maya and Callie. So, when I made an effort, things got better. Since I stopped making an effort, things have got worse. Maybe it is simpler than I thought. Meeting Katie was the best thing that happened to me and she made an effort to make me feel welcome. I haven't really taken her up on the offer properly, so tomorrow I will text her and ask her if she would be okay with me having lunch with them again.

As it's been a while since I heard from her I don't want to just assume. I really hope she says 'yes' though or I really will be back to square one but worse. Now I am worried about it. What if they say 'no'?

I won't be able to sleep now because I'll be worrying about it. Sod it, I'll text her now!

'Hey, r u ok if I join u all 4 lunch tomo? X'

What if she doesn't reply? What if she thinks I'm a complete idiot for asking about lunch when it's a whole day away? They probably do just think I'm a bitch who couldn't care less about people. I do care though! I just haven't really been showing it!

SHE REPLIED! She just said, 'Sure, bring a pic of R 4 Callie x.'

How easy was that? Now I will be able to sleep and at least I know that tomorrow won't be too bad at school because I have lunch to look forward to. Maybe they don't think I'm a bitch after all? I bet she has absolutely no idea how much that message meant to me. I just replied saying, 'Thanx, will do x,' and now I need to find a couple of good pictures of Reggie. That should keep me occupied for a while!

# Twenty-Six

If this had happened last week I think it would have pushed me over the edge. I feel stronger today. True to their word, Katie, Maya and Callie were okay with me having lunch with them again today. Callie has said that she'll do a picture of Reggie based on the photos I gave her. I couldn't pick just one so she's got plenty to choose from!

Maya wasn't so quiet today. 'I only joined this school a year ago,' she said, 'so I know it's pretty horrible. I don't envy you as I guess it's even worse when we're half way through all the exam stuff. I found it hard enough and I haven't had to do all the work in one year. I lost touch with most of the people from my old school because stuff just gets in the way. It's not the same when you're all in different parts of the country. I'm grateful for these two or I'd still be on my own having lunch and playing on my phone.'

That gave me the opportunity to say that I was sorry I hadn't been around for a while but I'd had the hockey trials and then was catching up with work. It was a lie but at least I had apologised! They didn't mind and when I said that I didn't make it onto the team, apparently I should be relieved. I didn't dare ask what they meant as I had a feeling it wouldn't help with my fear! I just smiled and agreed with them.

Maya was on a role with her story of moving. 'I moved for the same reasons as you but it was a lot more traumatic.' If only she knew. Katie had told her that we'd moved for my mum's job so she'd had the cover story. 'We moved because my mum had got a new job too, but the only reason she went for that job in the first place was because she'd hooked up with this guy on the internet. She packed me and my brother up, left my dad and we all moved in with this random guy.'

That did sound quite traumatic to be honest and I suddenly

felt very grateful that Mum hadn't tried to move a man into our house. I tried not to look too shocked and asked 'are you happy up here'?

'He's okay to be fair and Mum seems happy, but I do miss my old life sometimes.'

We shared a moment of understanding that didn't need words. We just looked at each other and I nodded in agreement. Katie broke the silence by announcing how lucky we both were to have met her! I can't disagree with that.

So lunch was great and I am so pleased that I sent that text last night. From then on the afternoon got worse and I actually ran home. Not only did I have a horrible afternoon, I realised how unfit I was too. As I was leaving the main hall after lunch I stopped to try and find my timetable as I had totally forgotten what room I needed to go to. Because Katie, Maya and Callie are in different classes I couldn't follow them. As I was checking the timetable I heard a voice say, 'She must be desperate if she's having lunch with them.

I looked up and there was the hockey girl that had tripped me up. She had a small group of girls with her and I recognised most of them from the trials day even though I've been trying to block it out. She just looked straight at me and I didn't know what she was going to do next. I was frozen to the spot and didn't know what to do. I knew that I needed to get out of the main hall so I put my timetable back in my bag and hoped that she wouldn't see my hand shaking.

I went to walk away and as I did she just laughed. She said, 'Girls like her aren't welcome on my team.' All the others laughed too and thankfully I got out of the main hall without any more comments.

What did she mean 'girls like me?' I was still shaking as I realised I had no idea where I was walking. I hadn't actually looked at which class I had next and now I would be late. I just needed to get to the classroom. I was so scared that they would find me and start saying stuff again. If I had been thinking logically then I would have guessed that they were already in their classroom as I was the only one standing in the playground at that point! I was grateful I couldn't see them, quickly checked the timetable and ran to class. I have done way too much running today. It's a good job I only played 20 minutes of hockey as any more might have killed me.

I apologised for being late and thankfully the teacher didn't question me about it. I just took my seat and kept my head down. When the bell went I was checking every direction to see whether I could see them, but I made it to the next class without any trouble. At the end of the day I didn't know what to do. There is only one exit so I had to go that way. I was terrified that I might see them. When I heard that bell I practically sprinted out of class, out of the building and through the exit. I ran home. I didn't look back. I am sure they didn't see me but what if they did? What did she mean by 'girls like me'? I have never been so pleased to see Reggie. I wasn't nervous taking him out for a walk, I knew that they wouldn't be heading to the park as they had hockey practice and I've never seen them there before! I never feel nervous with Reggie by my side. But what did they mean by 'girls like me'?

# Twenty-Seven

The little comments and digs have been going on for a few days now. It's like I'm constantly waiting for something, but I'm not sure what. I know it's not good though. They don't do anything major. It's just comments as I walk past. Most of the time I can't make out what they're saying. They just whisper to each other while they are looking at me. It's such a horrible feeling and yet I have no idea what to do about it. I almost wish that I knew what they were saying so that I knew what I was dealing with. Yesterday I'm pretty sure I heard one of them say, 'I wonder why she left her last school' and that scared me. I don't know if they could find out the truth, it wouldn't be that hard if they wanted to find out badly enough. What if they are trying to find out and what would they do if they did find out?

The thing is, I'm dreading going to school. The ache in the pit of my stomach is almost permanent now. At home I spend as much time as possible with Reggie and concentrate on getting my homework done. I have spent a lot of time this week dissecting *Silas Marner* for my English homework and haven't had the space in my brain to think about much else. Apparently there's a moral edge to the way the story is concluded and I have been finding 1000 words to explain how. Mum and I are getting on well, which is helping too. We had a rule when we first moved here that Reggie wouldn't be allowed in my room and that he'd learn that his space was downstairs. Every time she comes up to my room she overlooks the fact that Reggie is 'helping' with my homework! She never comes up empty handed either, tonight she brought a cuppa and some homemade banana cake, which is almost worth reading *Silas Marner* for. Apart from a half-hearted attempt to steal some cake, Reggie just lies there until it's time for him to go back downstairs to his own bed.

I don't feel unsafe at home; it's not like I think that all the hockey girls are going to show up at my front door. I just feel safer with Reggie with me! I think Mum's just relieved I'm getting on with my homework and if having Reggie up here makes that happen then it's a small price to pay. She sometimes makes little comments about needing to get the carpets cleaned but considering she has already spilt hair dye all over the bathroom carpet, Reggie should be the least of her carpet cleaning worries!

So, the evenings are okay. It's when it's time to go to bed that I start worrying about the next day. I plan the route around school, trying to work out where I could bump into them and figure out the best way to get to classes. Staying where there are lots of people has worked well so far. They can't all get around me like they did in the hall that day. It's a whisper as they walk past me. As I see them coming I can feel my heart beating faster and my hands go sweaty and cold. I keep saying to myself 'just keep walking, just keep walking' and it's over in seconds. It feels like a lifetime. I dread leaving lessons and I dread walking around the school. I feel sick as I'm starting to know when I'll have to walk past them.

Lunch breaks with Katie, Maya and Callie are brilliant but I hate leaving the main hall. I've started leaving a little bit early, telling them that I need the loo before my lesson. They probably think I have a weird stomach problem now! All of a sudden I'm disappearing off to the loo at the same time every day. I haven't told them about what is happening because I didn't want to tell them what was said when it all started. I don't think they'd care that much but I don't want to sound like I'm trying to stir anything up or making a drama out of nothing. I can't stop thinking about it though. I still don't know what they meant by 'girls like me' and I feel like I'll never hear the end of it. I have found out the name of the girl who seems to be leading the little pack. I saw her with the captain's arm band on after lunch yesterday, which means she's Nina Devlin.

I have no idea why she has decided that I'm worthy of all this attention. She must be really bored. I don't know what I have done to make her hate me this much. She doesn't know me, she doesn't know anything about me other than I wanted to play hockey. So that means it can't really be about me! If it's not about me then it must be about her. I wonder why she is so full of anger and hate. It's easy to think all this when I'm safely at home with my canine protector. It's not so easy when I'm at school trying to negotiate my way around the building like a secret agent who mustn't be spotted by the enemy. I think I've been watching too much TV!

I thought that I'd finished with having to overcome crappy times. I honestly thought that the worst thing that could ever happen had happened so surely everything else would be plain sailing. I don't know why these things are happening to me. I don't think I deserve it but I don't think anyone deserves it. It seems that life isn't that logical and sometimes crappy things can just happen. I didn't think there's be this many crappy things though! I know that if I can survive the rape then I can survive anything. I have survived so that makes me feel stronger. I just wish it wasn't about surviving any more. I wish it was just about having fun, enjoying life and being a 'normal' teenager. Whatever that is!

# Twenty-Eight

I think I may have crossed the line when it comes to normality. I have started talking to Reggie about what's going on at school. He hasn't come up with any bright ideas yet but he has given me his paw, rolled over and demanded a tummy rub. I'm not sure if that was a deliberate distraction technique for me but it worked! 'What would you do in this situation Reggie? Say you had a group of dogs who surrounded you in the park and said some pretty horrible things. Would you stand up to them, hide behind the tree or run away?' It made me smile and kept me occupied for ages. I am writing an essay for some homework about using pets as therapy. I would love to do that with Reggie but I'm not sure he's well behaved enough yet. I couldn't trust him to stay in one place or not be distracted by something he found more interesting. There are people who take their pets to visit people who are sick in hospital and stuff like that. Reggie almost took a man's walking stick in the park a couple of weeks ago as he must have thought the guy was only using it so he could play. Thankfully I caught him just in time and the man thought he was funny – that could have ended very badly! Maybe hospitals aren't the place for Reggie to hang out.

When I was doing the research I realised that Reggie has pretty much been my therapy since we moved here. I saw a counsellor for a while after it happened and I think she helped a bit, but Reggie has completely changed my life. I have a purpose and someone who needs me. I have a lot to thank him for and he has been the only real friend I've had since it happened. I know that my old friends were still around but it wasn't the same and since I've moved here I've been seriously lacking in the friends department. I guess that it might sound really sad but he's brilliant. I know that Mum is doing her best and she's working really hard to make sure we can live in this nice house and have nice things, but she's not here when I come home after school, Reggie is.

He just loves me. No matter how crappy the day has been (and they really are pretty crappy at the moment), I know that when I walk through the door he'll be pleased to see me. His tail can cause some serious bruising to the knees but it's amazing to see how happy he is just because I'm there. If I had to come home to an empty house I think that would push me over the edge. I'd have no reason to leave the house and nothing to motivate me to do anything. Maybe talking to Reggie about what's happening at school could put me into a 'crazy' category, but I don't care. Who else can I talk to about it? It's weird to think that I told Mum straight away after the rape but there's something stopping me telling her about this. Maybe it's because I know she's been through so much with me already. I don't want her to think that she did the wrong thing by us moving here. I don't want her to worry about me more than she already does. Maybe it's because I knew that I couldn't cope by myself before and this time I hope I can figure it out. It's not like I'm actually in danger or anyone else is in danger. It's just horrible. Well, it's more than horrible. I just don't know what I'd tell her as I think it sounds a bit childish. All they're doing is whispering and making comments in my direction. Mum would probably just tell me to ignore them – she would be right!

Reggie can't tell me to do anything though. It's quite nice in a way as I can talk and talk and talk without him interrupting. He just accepts me exactly as I am. Craziness and everything. When I'm out with Reggie it also means I sometimes get to talk to people. I usually have to apologise for Reggie running up to another dog or jumping all over little dogs, but dog owners are mostly nice people. They seem to understand that he's a big softy and they are very complimentary about how handsome he is. I know I'm slightly biased but he is the most handsome dog I have ever seen! Reggie's only goal in life is to make us happy. That's it and he does a very good job of it. I think we could learn a lot from that. What if the only reason we got up in the morning was to make someone else happy? What if we were pleased to see absolutely everyone we came into contact with? Maybe not to the extremes that Reggie goes to but just a smile wouldn't hurt! Wouldn't the world be a much nicer place? In one of the studies I read, it said that people who own pets are usually happier and healthier than people who don't. Maybe Nina Devlin doesn't have any pets and that's why she's so horrible! She certainly doesn't accept people for who they are and definitely isn't pleased to see anyone. Well, maybe her faithful clique but I haven't seen her smile at anyone else.

There's another study that says having a dog helps to reduce blood pressure. That has got to be true! When I come back from school I am really anxious. I've been on high alert all day and I can feel my heart beating faster when I see them or even when I think I might see them. It only takes a few minutes of being home with Reggie and I'm calm again. If I was home alone I think I'd carry on working myself up about it and I would be in a real mess. Nobody else can do that for me. I love Mum and feel really lucky that she's been so amazing but she can't do what Reggie does. Nobody can.

# Twenty-Nine

I feel so completely alone. I dread Mondays as that's when I know it will all start again. The week just becomes a countdown to Friday. It's nearly the Christmas holiday and that cannot get here quickly enough. That's the pattern now, just a weekly countdown and I can't see a way out of it. It's like no one cares and I'm pretty sure that no one has noticed. The way they do it is what gets me, they whisper it, they make sure only I can hear them. 'You lezzer, you dirty dyke', with Nina starting them off and then the rest of them joining in. I just need to write and get it out of my head as I don't know what else to do.

I'm embarrassed by what they're saying as I don't know what I have done to make them call me a lesbian. They say it as if it's the worst thing in the world and I just don't get it. I can see the others laughing and just want to scream, 'WHY ARE YOU DOING THIS TO ME?' but instead I just keep my head down and keep walking. Nina Devlin is the ringleader once again. She started it and her little sheep have followed. They can't think for themselves and it's as if they'll do anything she says just to make sure that it's not them on the receiving end of her words. They don't give a second thought to what it does to me. I don't matter to them.

I go from feeling really angry to really sad. I'm angry that they are doing this and also a little bit angry at myself for not standing up to them. Most of the time I feel sad that I don't have anywhere to turn. I am still having lunch with Katie, Maya and Callie, but I can't tell them what's going on. It's not like they could do anything to change what's happening and the lunch break is the only chance I have to think about other things. It's a relief just to talk about normal stuff without them knowing what's really happening. I wouldn't want them to start treating me differently. I also spend every waking moment thinking about it and enjoy the fact that the lunch break is also a break from my own head. Distraction helps me.

The first time that they said something was as I was leaving the loo after lunch a little while ago. I did my usual avoidance plan and went to the loo just before the lunch break ended. They must have spotted me and were waiting as I came back out onto the path. They just looked at me. At first they didn't say anything then Nina said, 'Lezzer,' in a loud whisper. I think I might have smiled. A tired, worn down half smile. My stomach turned, my heart started beating faster and I was physically shaking, but she did not see that. She was too busy looking around for backup. I wasn't smiling at what they were saying, but just because I thought that they had reached a new low with this one. Do they want to see me cry? I'm determined not to give them the satisfaction of seeing me upset. Do they want a response from me or do they want me to break down in front of them? Whatever they want, they are not getting it. I am stronger than they think. I just need to remind myself of that.

It's the powerlessness I hate more than anything. I've felt that before and didn't think I'd experience it again. Certainly not because of a group of girls my own age. I don't just mean the rape either. It was afterwards too. When Mum and I called the police it suddenly all was taken out of my hands. I have no idea what I would have done if it was left in my hands, but I did feel totally powerless and very frightened about what would happen next. It's like that now in some ways. I wake up every morning not sure what will happen.

When the police took over I was lucky that I had a really nice female police officer to help me. She was great and she did keep in touch throughout the whole court case. I just never knew when I would hear from her or what she'd tell me. I didn't know what would happen or what I was supposed to do. It's that fear of the unknown that I find so difficult to deal with. It's like that now, except I don't have a police team to back me up!

I wake up not knowing whether I'll have comments thrown in my direction or not. I spend all day worrying about whether I'll see them or not and then by the time I get home I'm knackered. On the very rare days that I don't see them, I don't even feel relieved any more. I just worry about the next day. I am struggling to concentrate and that's not helping me either. Even burying myself in *Silas Marner* won't help at the moment! I'm much more likely to bury myself in a box of Jaffa Cakes. If I don't pass my exams then all this will be for nothing. I could have stayed at my old school, felt a bit crap and failed my exams! I can't wait for the Christmas holiday now. Some time away from school, time with Mum and Reggie and time to just forget about all the crap that's going on. Not long now and this year will be over!

# Thirty

I have literally never been happier to see the last day of term. I feel like a weight has been lifted from my shoulders and I can breathe again. I had a chat with Miss Haywood in registration today as she wanted to check how I had done this term. She said that the teachers were pleased with how I'd been catching up. They are either very easily impressed or I've done better than I thought! She also said that I was very quiet around school and asked if I'd been making friends and settling in okay. I just said 'yes' and that I'm okay. What was I supposed to say to that?

*Well actually Miss Haywood there are a few girls who are making my life a living hell as they call me a lesbian (although not that politely) at every opportunity as if that is the crime of the century and I deserve to be punished on a daily basis. I don't know why they have chosen to focus on me but it seems that their tiny minds can't deal with actual conversation and they can only let out one word at a time and only then with the backing of at least five other girls, who must all laugh on cue. They can only do this when they know that I am on my own because that's the sort of brave soldiers they are, and won't ever actually ask me anything or dare to speak to me directly. Other than that, I'm having the time of my life. Thanks for asking.*

I wonder what she would have said to that?! I feel a bit better for having a little rant but it's a shame I have only written it down rather than actually saying it out loud. At least I'm doing okay with the schoolwork. If I'd been failing there too then Nina and her merry gang of gigglers would really be winning.

I thought that they had started to get the better of me. I was waking up in the middle of the night, coming up with illnesses I could have that would mean I wouldn't be able to go to school. I have a whole list of great ideas that I could work on. Drama has never been something I am very good at, but I have even practised faking some of the symptoms. I knew that it must be bad when I was faking stomach pains up in my room to see how realistic I could make them. That's pretty sad and desperate! I know that Mum would have seen straight through it, and even if she didn't I'm pretty sure a doctor would have done! The desire to just not go to school had become overwhelming and I would have done almost anything to stay at home.

I am stuck every day with a battle going on in my head. I want to succeed and I want to do well. I want to pass my exams and have good grades. I want Mum to be proud of me and I want to be proud of myself. At the same time I want to shut out the whole world (well, Nina) and stay in bed. If I think about Nina and her gigglers too much then the desire to stay in bed with my fake stomach pains becomes much stronger. I feel like the odds are stacked against me and nothing I do will make things better. If I think about walking out of school in July, having done my best in all my exams, then somehow the day becomes more bearable.

I have a little film in my head of Mum dropping me off in August to pick up my exam results. We have started the day with a great breakfast and taken Reggie for a long walk. He's been his usual self, the sun is shining and I am nervous about going into school and opening that envelope. Mum is doing her best to distract me, but we both know it's not working. We drive to school so that we can go straight out for lunch afterwards as Mum has planned the whole day. She booked her time off work as soon as she knew when the results would be out and decided that whatever happened we would have a great day together! So, we're at school and as I get out of the car she just tells me that she loves me and that she is really proud of me. I hope that she still feels that way when I get back in the car! I walk into the main hall without a second thought, nobody says anything to me and I am actually feeling quite relaxed. I keep reminding myself that I did my best and that's all I could have done. I walk to the desk and it's Miss Haywood who hands me my envelope. I want to tear it open but I take it outside. I walk to the car. I get in. Mum looks at me, desperate to know how I did. She sees the sealed envelope and smiles. She gently asks me to open it. I have got all As and Bs with one C in Maths! We both cry! Mum laughs at me when I tell her that I worked harder for that C in Maths than anything else.

That's where the film ends. Who cares what happens next! I know that everything will be okay no matter what happens next. Concentrating on that becoming a reality is what is getting me through. Just thinking about that day and what will happen has made sure I haven't used my fake stomach ache and it's meant that I've done okay in catching up with the school work. It has kept me focused. Whenever I don't want to go to school I play that film in my head. Once I've done that, I know what I need to do.

Now, I'm looking forward to telling Mum what Miss Haywood said and enjoying a few days with no hassle and lots of time at home.

# Thirty-One

Happy New Year!

I can't say I'm sad to see the back of last year. It wasn't all bad I suppose and getting Reggie was definitely the highlight but it's time to start thinking about making the most of this year now. The Christmas break has been brilliant and I've loved not being at school. The stupid thing is I've probably got more work done in the last week than I'd have got done if I was in school and I actually wanted to do it. I have been so relaxed. It's amazing to wake up in the morning and not be frightened about what the day might bring. I can just be myself and not worry about what I am doing, saying or who I am looking at. I didn't realise how preoccupied I had become. I was so overwhelmed by the fear of bumping into Nina and the gigglers that I didn't notice everything else that I had started to worry about. I have been worried about saying the wrong thing or looking at the wrong person just in case it starts even more people off with calling me names or making comments. No wonder I was completely exhausted.

Christmas Day was great as it was just Mum and me. We went for a long walk with Reggie and then came home to open our presents. We were like children. Excitedly ripping off the paper and then screwing it into a ball to throw at Reggie. We ate chocolate for breakfast and didn't start preparing the dinner until the afternoon because we felt a bit sick. This was the first Christmas that we have had this much fun as we used to spend Christmas Day with my grandparents. We had to go to church in the morning, which always put a downer on the day. I know that it's the whole point of Christmas, but we didn't go any other day of the year so I never really understood why we had to go then. They also insisted we wore our 'best' clothes and every year I was told that 'best' and 'favourite' were two very different things. Anyway, it was really nice to just do what we wanted to do even though Mum mentioned more than once that she felt a bit guilty for not going! She didn't feel guilty enough to actually go thankfully!

I was really excited as for the first time I got Mum a present that was a surprise because she didn't have to give me the money to buy it! She did give me some money and I bought her some perfume, but she wasn't expecting the second present. It's all thanks to Callie. She drew the picture of Reggie for me and it is absolutely amazing. Now there's another good thing to have come out of last year. My three lunchtime friends! I am so grateful to Callie as it must have taken her ages. It's a pencil drawing of him lying down in our living room and she has got every detail just right. Even the design on his collar and the way his tongue is sticking out very slightly. I asked her to sign the corner as I'm pretty sure she'll be rich and famous one day. She was really chuffed that I asked her to sign it as I was the first person to say that! It was nice to be able to show her how much I appreciated it. I bought a frame and wrapped it up, I almost couldn't wait until Christmas day, but I'm glad I did. Mum cried! I'm not sure if she was happier with the picture or the fact that I'd made friends!

I had some new clothes, CDs and the obligatory selection box. Even though I think I might be getting too old for one of those it doesn't stop me wanting to open it straight away and then getting told I'll spoil my dinner! Never mind the fact we'd cracked open the Roses at dawn and had been fighting over the last strawberry one. Dinner was delicious and we needed another walk to make sure we had room for pudding. True to recent form, I could eat non-stop. I am constantly reaching for something to eat so all the Christmas food was a bonus. Reggie did well with treats and his own Christmas dinner. He was left unattended for five minutes and decided to help himself to the leftovers too! It's amazing how much that dog can eat! Watching crap TV and stuffing ourselves with even more chocolate took up the rest of the evening. We only had one tiny falling out over the music. Mum kept telling me to turn it down and I shouted back that she shouldn't have bought them for me if she didn't want me to play them. I felt bad though as I know money is tight and Mum had saved to get them for me! I turned it down and went to help peel potatoes! Well done me!

The Boxing Day visit from the grandparents went well. They asked if we had found a church to go to and just as Mum said, 'No, I don't think there's one near here,' we heard the bells from the local church start ringing. Oops! That made me laugh a lot but I don't think Grandma found it very funny! It was a nice day though; they brought presents for us and even wrapped up two presents for Reggie. I think they enjoyed seeing him more than us. I don't blame them! They were making a real effort and asking me about school and how I was feeling about the exams. It was nice to just get normal questions. We managed a whole day without talking about what had happened. When they left Mum and I were both impressed with how the day had gone.

Mum's been impressed with how I've been doing some homework every day so it's meant she's also had some time to herself to relax. She's been taking Reggie out for long walks and then we have had afternoons and evenings together. We even met up with Jenny, Katie and Bailey which was great. This afternoon has been spent tidying up ready for Jane as she's coming to stay for a couple of days before I go back to school and Mum goes back to work. I am not thinking about that yet though. It is still the holidays and I'm not letting any thoughts of school spoil it!

# Thirty-Two

The Christmas and New Year bubble has been burst...by Jane of all people. I know that I haven't been coping too well with everything that has been going on but at the same time I thought I was doing okay. I have been keeping up to date with schoolwork, Reggie has never missed a walk and I haven't let Nina and the gigglers completely get the better of me. That's without everything else. I think I'm doing more than okay actually! I can even say that I have friends in Katie, Maya and Callie, which is more than I could say last time I saw Jane. Right now, it feels like Mum and Jane have it in for me too.

We were all sitting having a cuppa before bed (of course) and Jane had brought some homemade banana cake with her as it's my favourite. I was half way through my second piece – I'm not greedy, it's just really good cake – and Jane asked whether I had thought about taking up sport again. I could see the look in her eyes. She was really saying that I should do something about the weight I've put on.

I'm not stupid. I know that I have put on a bit of weight. My favourite old jeans don't fit and my new Christmas clothes were a size bigger than usual. When I'm at home I tell myself that I have to wear my jogging bottoms and baggy tops because of taking Reggie out. It's not true. They are the only things that fit. I started to get upset and said that she knew what had happened with hockey so what did she expect me to do. I had gone from being really active to doing nothing except walking the dog and eating.

Comfort eating is something I have only done since I was raped. The counsellor talked to me about it a bit when I turned up for a session clutching a packet of biscuits. Before, I was really happy and always busy so food was just something that featured throughout the day and I didn't really think about it. When I started spending more time at home, it became a distraction. I think that calling it 'comfort eating' is a bit misleading though because I didn't really get any 'comfort'! I was occupied whilst I was eating then when I'd finished I just felt full and annoyed with myself. That's not comforting at all. I have been eating more since Nina and the gigglers have been making my life miserable. It's a bad habit more than anything. I don't choose healthy food, I go for sugar. Then I feel rubbish! It's not a great idea! The counsellor drew the cycle out for me in that session and I could see how ridiculous it was. I'm sitting here now with a bowl full of grapes and a Kit Kat, I know exactly which one should be my next snack, but I won't pretend it's going to happen. I'm sure that Jane could come up with a million theories about why I'm doing it and I'm sure that she'd be right with everything she said. There is, however, one simple fact – when I was eating healthily and exercising I felt great and looked much better than I do now. I need to break the habit of choosing to eat sugary crap and replace it with good stuff. It's not rocket science! I know that I need to exercise too. Not just because of my weight but because I felt so much better when I did. It sounds so easy when I say it like this!

Jane asked why I had turned to food. Hmmm. I just said that I was stressed about schoolwork, didn't have many friends and was worried about the exams. I didn't dare tell her what I was being called! Jane is a lesbian so I had a feeling she would march into school offering to do lessons on inclusion and equality and make the whole situation a million times worse! Who knows, it might have made the situation a million times better, but I'm not prepared to take the risk! I didn't want to upset her either. Jane is one of the most amazing people I know (even though she has annoyed me today!) and I think she'd be gutted if she knew I was being called a dyke. She has faced some discrimination in her lifetime so she knows how horrible it is, and because she is so protective of me I know she'd be upset and angry about what was being said. It's funny because when I was first called a dyke that day outside the toilets I smiled because I thought of Jane! I thought that if I was half as successful and fabulous as her, then being a dyke could only be a good thing!

They both started going on and on about how now it's the New Year it's a great time to start thinking about eating more healthily and taking more exercise. Mum started listing all the healthy things she could cook (that didn't take long) and how we needed to cut down on takeaways and puddings. Then she started making a shopping list to make sure that I had healthy packed lunches and said I could drink water rather than squash. Great! As if the school day needed to get any more painful! She said that when we have nice dry days we could take the bikes out or we could start jogging! Jogging?! If I start running when I'm out with Reggie he thinks it's a game and usually starts running around in circles looking like he's lost his mind! I don't think that's going to help anyone.

Right now though, I don't get why they can't just leave me alone to enjoy the holiday. It's not like I'm refusing to leave the house and constantly eating. I hate the fact I'm getting bigger without them pointing it out and coming up with a million plans around how to make me fit and healthy in record time. I thought that we were going to have a nice couple of days but now I feel like I'm being targeted at home too. It's the last thing I need. I came upstairs and left them to it down there. I even left my second piece of cake, which I think made my point!

# Thirty-Three

Okay, I've had a sleep, calmed down and thought about what Mum and Jane were saying yesterday. I guess they're right. I have put on weight, I am turning to food and I am not happy about it. I haven't put on a massive amount but I do wish I could still fit in to my favourite jeans and I wish I didn't get out of breath walking up the stairs.

I know that I said that I'm not choosing healthy food but it's more than that. I am almost craving the bad stuff. I'm eating crisps, sweets, chocolate and biscuits almost every day. I never used to do that and I know that it's pretty disgusting. I know that it doesn't really bring me 'comfort' either, but it's as if I need it. When I think about it, I only seem to reach for those types of food when I have had a really bad day. I don't do it at weekends and although I have eaten quite a lot of chocolate over Christmas (that's the rule isn't it?!), I haven't felt like I needed it in the same way I do after a bad day.

When I come home from school I usually feel awful. I've been completely powerless all day and I've been on high alert. I'm totally knackered by the time I get home and just feel drained. The stupid thing is that 'comfort' eating has actually made me more stressed. Not only do I feel like crap in the first place, I then eat and feel worse!

At school I am often too nervous to eat very much too. By the time I have lunch I'm more preoccupied with looking for Nina and the gigglers to think about eating. I race home at the speed of an unfit tortoise and just stuff my face with the first thing I find. Well, that's not true as the first thing I see is the fruit in the fruit bowl! Somehow an apple doesn't really tempt me and so I head for the chocolate and biscuits. Before, I would happily have an apple when I came in from school and wouldn't even think about eating loads of crappy stuff. That was when I felt okay about myself though. I didn't worry about how I looked or what people said. I think that's because I looked okay and I don't think anyone ever really said anything mean. I didn't realise how lucky I was! I know that there's no point wishing I could turn the clock back as it's pointless, but sometimes I really wish I could.

It has got a lot worse recently and if I don't do something about it I'll end up needing the fire brigade to come and help me out of the house! I saw a programme where that actually happened and I was laughing, wondering anyone could let themselves get so big. Maybe I now know how it can start. The more I sit around doing nothing (other than watching fat people on TV), the less I feel like doing. The only thing I want to do that involves moving is taking Reggie out. I definitely feel better when I do that but I think it's also because I feel like I'm going out with a friend. It's fun and I feel safe. What else can I do where I feel like that? A bit of PE at school isn't making any difference and I'm not really making an effort there because I want to try and stay invisible.

I feel like I have almost given up. I'm doing enough to get by and enough to get my grades but that's it. I think that idea in my head that life would be plain sailing after everything that happened was very, very wrong. I remember all of those cards that I read just before I moved where people were praising me for being inspirational. What would they be saying if they could see me now? I didn't let the rapist completely defeat me as I made sure he paid the price and was sent to prison, but I am letting a group of girls get the better of me. A group of girls. That's all they are. Just the thought of them and the thought of going back to school is making me want to reach for the biscuits. Is that the only thing I have control over now – what I eat? As soon as I think of them I feel powerless. Maybe that's the difference. I did something about the man who raped me. I stood up for myself. I needed a lot of help to do that but I did it. I was proud of myself for doing it too. I didn't have time to think about biscuits because

I was busy thinking about what was happening and how I had played a part in making the world a little bit safer. It was the hardest thing I have ever done but I wouldn't change the fact that I told someone.

Is it that simple? What if I did tell someone?

Surely all I need to do is keep my head down and just get on with the next two terms. Two more terms of this? I don't know if I can take two more terms of this. I don't think just eating healthily and taking more exercise is going to work to fix the problem either. I know that I will feel better about myself and that I need to do those things to help myself, but I need to do something more. I need to actually DO SOMETHING about those girls and the way they're treating me. I suppose they are just bullies. I never thought I'd be bullied. They think they are powerful because I am letting them get away with it. I am letting them make me feel like crap. I don't want to feel like crap anymore!

# Thirty-Four

'So, they think I'm a lesbian,' I blurted out as I saw Jane this morning.

She just listened, she did not say a word until I had finished. We must have walked for miles and I couldn't stop talking. After my announcement this morning we grabbed the keys, started walking and everything came spilling out. I felt so relieved. When I finally stopped and she was completely up to date she hugged me. I cried!

She was gutted about the whole lesbian thing, but thankfully didn't mention anything about coming into school! I told her that I thought of her when they called me a lezzer and a dyke and that she was an amazing role model to me. She cried! 'I had a role model at school,' she said. 'She was the deputy head teacher, a firm but fair woman who never took any nonsense. She got me through some really bad times because she had faith in me and could see something in me that others couldn't see. If it wasn't for her I could have taken a very different path. I've been meaning to write and say thank you for years. You know what, I'm going to write to her. If I can do that same thing for you and help to you to see that there's so much more to you than what's happening now then that makes me really happy.'

We talked about when I was at my happiest. 'It's when I'm out with Reggie, away from school, I love it when it's just me and him. I feel safe, he makes me laugh and he's just happy to be with me. He doesn't let me sit around feeling sorry for myself and even if I'm at my worst, he is still happy to see me. He loves me unconditionally and I don't have to pretend to be something I'm not. I don't have to pretend to be happy or okay, yet when I'm with him I become happy and okay very quickly! I'm happy at home with Mum too, it's just that I'm often preoccupied with worrying about school and that probably means I'm a bit of a pain in the arse to be around. I enjoy having lunch with Katie, Maya and Callie so it's not as if everything is horrible.'

She was impressed that I wasn't saying everything was crap and I think she's pleased I'm having human contact and not just talking to the dog!

'Think back to before the rape,' she said. 'When were you at your happiest back then and what made you happy back then?'

It feels like a lifetime ago. As I was thinking back to my old life it didn't even feel like it was me I was thinking about. It is a totally different version of 'me' in every sense. In comparison to now, everything about that time was happier. She wouldn't let me get away with 'everything' as an answer though.

She kept on asking because I was only saying 'everything'! All of a sudden it was as if a light bulb had switched on in my brain. I knew exactly when I was happiest back then. 'When I was doing sport!' I used to do anything and everything that was on offer and I was all right at most things. I loved the feeling of being active, of having a bit of competition and just pushing myself to see if I could get better. I was around other people and I used to be really confident. I took it all for granted and that confident person has almost disappeared. The person who would try anything and be the first to do any dare that was presented to her was long gone. In her place was someone who was frightened of going to school and was just getting through each day with the help of a dog! A gorgeous dog, but still a dog!

I don't want to carry on like this. I'm fed up. Completely and utterly fed up.

She asked how I would feel if I could have double the happiness – still take Reggie out and then some evenings and maybe at the weekend also do some sport.

Sure, the idea of it sounds brilliant, but that will mean actually starting something new and also doing all my exams. She said that she knows it's an important year at school but a bit of time doing some exercise would help me. I was excited at the thought of it but terrified at the same time. I knew that I didn't want to do anything linked to school. Jane agreed and said that it would be nice for me to join something that was completely separate from school so that I could meet new people. I laughed; meeting new people wasn't going very well for me at the moment! She reminded me that I'd met three new people who I enjoyed spending time with – fair point! I have promised Jane that by the end of the holidays I will have found a local club that I want to join and I'll call her to tell her about it.

Jane has also made a promise. She won't tell Mum what we talked about. She has only promised that because we will talk regularly and I will always tell her the truth. I just don't want Mum to worry and I already feel a million times better just by telling Jane what is happening. I have a plan now. I am going to find a sport that I can do in the evenings that won't get in the way of walking Reggie and will help me to feel better. I'm secretly quite excited about it!

# Thirty-Five

I did it! It's the last day of the holiday and I have decided what I want to do. I am going to learn Taekwondo! I have always wanted to do martial arts as I thought it would be cool to say I've got a black belt. I really like the idea of learning to defend myself too. I was walking back from the park when I saw a poster, there were pictures of girls taking part too so I figured it would be okay for me. The place where the classes are is near home and the sessions are later on in the evening so I can take Reggie, have something to eat and it won't be too late if I also need to do some homework!

I called Jane and told her about it. She was impressed and said that I could think about Nina and the gigglers when I was learning to punch properly! That thought had crossed my mind a few times too. She was proud when I told her that I'd been on a mission. I have already emailed them to find out when I can start and I've arranged with Mum to have a lift. Their website says that it doesn't matter how fit you are and that they'll work with anyone who wants to take it up. There's a picture of a woman doing a flying kick and I would really like to learn how to do that! I think that it will help me lose weight and also mean that I want to eat more healthily so that I can do it properly. I'm sure that if I turn up after having eaten a packet of biscuits I'd just be sick! I am hoping that I don't see anyone from school when I go there, but I get the first lesson as a trial so if I don't like it I never have to go back again. As soon as I get an email back I'll know when I can start. I'm trying very hard not to check my emails every thirty seconds!

Spending a couple of days looking at clubs has kept me occupied. I'm going back to school tomorrow and until this evening I hadn't even thought about it. I'm less nervous about starting Taekwondo than I am about going back to school!

Meeting new people doesn't seem as scary as going back to a place where you know the people don't like you. I've had a message from Katie saying they'll be in the main hall for lunch, so at least I know I'll be seeing them. It's not like everyone hates me I suppose, it just feels that way a lot of the time.

I am dreading it, but I also know that it has to be done. I hope that they'll all be busy talking about their holidays and will have forgotten all about me, but I think that might be wishful thinking! I feel stronger since I have told Jane about it but now I wish she was coming in to school with me. She wouldn't let them get away with what they're doing to me. When I was talking to her on the phone she asked if I was still writing in the journal. I told her that I was but maybe not as often as I should. I told her that it helped when I did write in it though! She said that I should use it as often as I could and she also asked me to do three more things with my journal from now on:

1. Write down three goals that I have.
2. Write down the successes I have had that day.
3. Write down all the things I am grateful for.

We stayed on the phone for ages talking about it and I am starting the way I mean to go on!

My three goals are all going to happen this year and they are…

- It is April and I have my first belt in Taekwondo.
- It is August and I have passed all of my exams.
- It is September and I have decided what I want to do next in my life.

The first two were pretty easy to come up with but I couldn't think of third one for ages. Jane kept asking me questions about what mattered most to me and I realised that I had no idea what

I wanted to do with my life. I just know that I want to do something that matters, something that makes a difference. I have a while to think about it!

The successes I have had today:

- Emailing the Taekwondo club and deciding that's what I want to do (maybe I should count that as two?!).
- Taking Reggie out for a two hour walk and he didn't misbehave once (maybe that's his success, not mine?!).
- I have got everything ready for school tomorrow and all my homework and coursework done.

That's not too bad I think! According to Jane, thinking about the things that have gone well will help me to focus on the good stuff and not on the crappy stuff with Nina and the gigglers. It's working at the moment but that's easy to say when I'm away from school.

The things I am grateful for today:

- Reggie!
- Talking to Jane.
- Mum (most of the time).
- Having the day off school.
- It wasn't raining when we went out for a walk with Reggie.

That's about it! Jane said that this will make me happier just by writing it down. I'm not sure how it will work, but Jane's usually right so I'll give it a go! She said it doesn't matter what goes on the list, it can be something really small or something really big...as long as I'm grateful for it. She said that she does this every day. I said I'd try but we both agreed that it might be a little bit optimistic!

# Thirty-Six

They kicked off again.

I've not had one day of peace.

The whispering as they walked past me has become louder and now they have started to bump into me in corridors. One of the gigglers has found her voice and started laughing when Nina bumped into me this morning saying that I probably liked it. Yeah...bloody loved it. Being laughed at, pushed and called a dyke is brilliant...loving every second of it. I must double check with Jane whether it's every lesbian's dream to be pushed by an idiot! Hmmm...I think I know what she'll say. At least I know I can talk to her about it now and that makes me feel a little bit stronger.

To make it even worse, I had a test in Maths. I knew that it was happening today so I had revised and prepared as much as I could. It was on the way to Maths that Nina bumped into me. I was really shaken up by the time I got to class and couldn't get my head around the questions at all. It was like my brain had just switched off. I usually find Maths difficult anyway, but this was something else. I remember one of the questions was asking me to work out the area of a triangle. Why? Why would I ever need to work out the area of a triangle in my day to day life? I just couldn't concentrate and my mind was completely blank. I had even revised how to do this, but all of a sudden it became impossible as I was thinking about what had happened in the corridor and why I needed to be able to work out the area of a triangle!

I did the best I could but once again I had let them get the better of me. I am angry with myself more than anything. I am freaked out that they have started to get physical but it's still the way they speak to me...well, speak *at* me – that hurts the most. That doesn't mean that I'm going to fail because of them though. Even though I can't see the point, there is something weirdly satisfying about being able to answer Maths questions and I hate it when I've revised and then mess it up!

I came home and fell into my routine, I took Reggie out first. I came home and just ate and ate and ate. I couldn't help myself. I've been trying so hard to break the habit but today I just couldn't do it. Now I feel sick and even more annoyed with myself.

I have just looked at the goals I wrote down at the end of the holidays and they feel completely impossible. It's my first night at Taekwondo tomorrow and the way I feel right now, I don't want to go. I'm not sure it's worth the risk of meeting more people who might hate me. At least I wouldn't have to go back again I suppose, not like school. Jane told me that it's on days like this when I feel really crap that I should make more effort to write everything that she said. I can't believe she does this every day! Although, maybe that's why she's done so well!

My three goals are...

- It is April and I have my first belt in Taekwondo.
- It is August and I have passed all of my exams.
- It is September and I have decided what I want to do next in my life.

I still want to do these things. After today it just feels so hard. I want to go to Taekwondo but I'm scared. I obviously want to pass my exams, but if the Maths test is anything to go by I need to do a lot of work to stay in control of my thoughts and emotions. What if they come up to me just before one of the proper exams? What would I do then?

The successes I have had today:

- I didn't cry when Nina bumped in to me...I am counting that as a success!
- I still tried to answer the questions in the test even though

my head was making it really difficult.

Two successes. I didn't think I'd be able to come with any!

The things I am grateful for today:

- Reggie!
- Getting home in one piece.

Just two things there too. Trying to be positive and grateful when all I want to do is curl up in bed is not easy, so at least I have written them down. That's more than I've done for the last two weeks.

I've got all my stuff ready for tomorrow evening so that I don't have any excuses not to go to Taekwondo. Mum is finishing work early so we can take Reggie and have dinner together before I go. She said she'll either stay and watch or sit in the car and wait, whatever I'd prefer! I'd quite like her to watch, but not if she's the only one there. When I wrote the goal down and thought about having my first belt I felt a bit excited again. I do want to go. The guy who emailed me is going to meet me at the door and go through some information with me first, so at least I don't have to just walk in when I have no idea what to do. Mum and I both agree that any sport that encourages you to wear pyjamas has got to be worth a try! I don't think I'll be saying that to the people with the black belts though!

# Thirty-Seven

Taekwondo rocks.

I am absolutely knackered and I think every single part of me is aching but I have not felt this happy in ages!

School was the same as always. The comments were thrown in my direction and I just kept my head down and tried to hide the fact they were really getting to me. I am not sure why I bother avoiding eye contact with them as they say what they want and do when they want regardless. Nina bumped into me again and at that moment I knew that I would be going to Taekwondo. It's not that I had any great ambitions to throw her across the corridor or anything (although that might be fun!), but I want to know that I can defend myself if I need to. I want to feel stronger as at the moment I feel very vulnerable. It was another long day, only made better by lunch and the thought of going home. I didn't tell Katie, Maya and Callie about the plans to start Taekwondo as I didn't want to turn around in a couple of days and say I wasn't going back, or tell them that I'd been too scared to go in the first place. I don't think they'd have cared either way but I'd have been really embarrassed.

I raced home so that I could have some time with Reggie before leaving. 'What do you think Reggie? To go or not to go, that is the question? I want to go, I want to learn that high kick, maybe not tonight but it would be cool one day. What if they're all horrible and it's just like school? What if I walk in there and they all just stare at me? What if they're not horrible and I actually find people I can talk to? If I don't go I'll just be annoyed with myself. I can just go this once, right? If I hate it then I never have to go again? Why doesn't school work that way? Right, I'm going, thanks Reggie.' Decision made. If there was anything that I didn't like or anything that was said then I would never have to go back. So, all I had to do when I got home was eat my dinner, get changed into the stuff that I had got ready and get in the car. I didn't even have to walk! That sounded much easier…three little steps.

Reggie was a big help as he didn't run off or go chasing after another dog so I managed to get home on time. I think Mum had been reading up on healthy energy filled foods again as I warmed up the chicken and brown rice dinner that was in the fridge! I even resisted the urge to crack open a new packet of custard creams – well done me. That is definitely a success for today!

Looking at the clothes I'd got ready made me realise just how much I'd let myself get into really bad habits. I had a new sports kit that Mum bought me. It was two sizes bigger than the kit I had when we moved here. I used to laugh at people who had really big sports kit. I thought that if they were really doing sport they wouldn't need the bigger sizes! I really hoped that people wouldn't be saying that about me. At least I am doing something about it now before I get even bigger. I am not going to let that happen.

Mum came home on time and was all set to take me. After only a few minutes of talking myself in and out of going I got in the car. I even remembered my bottle of water! I felt really nervous on the way there and even though I knew it wasn't far away it was the quickest journey of my life. Before I knew it we were getting out of the car and I was walking through the front doors. As promised, the instructor was waiting for us and there was no turning back. We filled in the forms and he invited Mum to sit and watch with some of the other parents. I was pleased she was there and very pleased that she wasn't the only one!

I had so much fun. It was difficult and definitely showed me how unfit I had become (not that I needed another reminder!), but everyone was nice to me and I wasn't the only new kid. As soon as we'd finished I asked Mum if I could sign up. I know it is more money and I said I'd get a job, but she just smiled and said she'd already signed me up! I already can't wait to go back and will be practising the moves. I don't want to have the white belt for long!

My three goals are...

- It is April and I have my first belt in Taekwondo.
- It is August and I have passed all of my exams.
- It is September and I have decided what I want to do next in my life.

After this evening, all of these things feel doable!

The successes I have had today:

- I stayed away from the custard creams!
- I went to Taekwondo and didn't talk myself out of it.
- I gave 100 per cent while I was at Taekwondo even though I'm sure I won't be able to walk in the morning!

The things I am grateful for today:

- Reggie!
- Mum supporting me in going to Taekwondo.
- People being welcoming at Taekwondo and not being the only new girl.

Today has been a good day (well...this evening has been good!).

# Thirty-Eight

I got my first belt in Taekwondo tonight and I just had to write it down! I have actually been successful in something and achieved something!

Everything at school has been carrying on the way it always has but sod them, I've got my belt. Nina and the gaggle haven't given up on calling me a lezzer at every opportunity and I still dread going into school, but it just doesn't occupy all of my thoughts any more. I know that when I leave that place I have great things going on. Nobody from school goes to the training sessions. It's my thing and nobody can take it away from me. When I walk down the corridors now, I don't always hang my head in fear and shame. I look up and in my head imagine delivering that flying kick straight into the gaggle. When they bump into me I almost smile to myself (not that I'd ever let them see that!) as I know that I'm learning ways to stop them doing that. I don't think I'd ever use the moves I've learnt but just knowing that I can is a really cool feeling. I don't know what I can do to make them stop and I've pretty much resigned myself to the fact that this is it until after the exams. I just need to do my work, get through each day and concentrate on the good stuff. As soon as that school bell goes I am out of there. Since I started Taekwondo I have been concentrating better in class so I think I'm doing okay and am up to date with all the work I needed to catch up on. That's a relief as there was just so much to do. Now I only have to do the homework that's set for everybody and not do double because I'm catching up too. I didn't think I'd ever be able to catch up but it is amazing what I've been able to do since I started actually concentrating and just getting on with it rather than finding a million excuses why it couldn't be done.

Last weekend, we had a family outing with Katie and co. What was supposed to be a quiet picnic with the dogs turned into a bit of a nightmare. Bailey and Reggie clearly weren't keen on the dog treats we'd brought for them and when they realised they weren't allowed any of our chicken salad (yep, the healthy eating plan continues), they ran off to another family and returned with pork pies. That family were not dog fans so Mum and Jenny had to go and apologise, while Katie and I were in tears with laughter trying to wrestle the pork pies out of their mouths. At least Reggie was tired. I'm getting on really well with Katie, but I still haven't told her about what goes on at school. It's nice to talk about normal stuff and, for me, that's a break from thinking about school stuff! I have been into town with her, Maya and Callie too which was a lot of fun. I was looking around me quite a lot though as I was a bit scared we'd bump into Nina and the gaggle. Thankfully that didn't happen! I'm not sure if those three really have other friends either as they're always together. I haven't seen them with anyone else and they don't really talk about seeing other friends. Maybe I'm not the only one who has been having trouble making friends! At least they have each other and I'm grateful that they have included me. I don't think I'd be able to get through school without them. They have absolutely no idea that they have been a lifeline for me! Maybe I'll tell them at the end of the school year and say thank you!

The evenings have started to fly by as I'm either doing Taekwondo or making sure I have all my homework done. Once I've taken Reggie for his walk, eaten and done what I needed to do that evening I am knackered. The weird thing is, even though I'm busier, I'm getting more stuff done than before! I used to sit at home, making excuses and not doing as much homework as I could have been doing. Now that I have to fit in Taekwondo sessions and practice I am making time to do my homework too. One of the teachers said to me recently that if I was really struggling to get everything done I could think about repeating the year to get the grades I was capable of! That was enough to make me work doubly hard as I am never setting foot in that school again once I have my results. I will do whatever it takes to make sure I pass.

The bonus is I am losing weight too! All the exercise and no time for snacking means that I'm eating healthy meals and looking better too. I've still got a way to go but I'm doing okay and feeling good. I'm not out of breath walking up the stairs and chasing Reggie around the park is fun again!

My three goals are…

- It is April and I have my first belt in Taekwondo.
- It is August and I have passed all of my exams.
- It is September and I have decided what I want to do next in my life.

OH YES! First goal has been achieved and it's only March! I need to update that now!

- It is June and I have my second belt in Taekwondo!

The successes I have had today:

- I got my first belt! I passed and I achieved my goal!
- I think that's more than enough for one day! I think there have been other successes over the last two months so well done me!

The things I am grateful for today:

- Reggie!
- The support of my new friends at Taekwondo.
- Having this journal and being able to write about something good!

# Thirty-Nine

So, they pinned me up against a wall, called me all the names under the sun and wouldn't let me go.

I was just about to leave and go home as quickly as I could. I had packed up my bag and as usual slipped past the crowds heading slowly for the gate. There was never anything slow about my journey home. Just before the gates, there is a small alleyway leading to the science block. They were waiting. I don't know if they know my name or whether they think I'm actually called 'Oi Lezzer', but they shouted and then blocked my path. I was shoved into the alleyway where they pinned me against the wall. They were literally screaming in my face. What had I done to make them this angry? I didn't know what they were going to do to me. That was the worst thing. The fear. After what felt like a lifetime they let me go. I ran. I ran home. Just like before.

It all came flooding back. That feeling of helplessness, complete and utter helplessness. The fear was completely overwhelming. Why today? Why me? Why didn't anyone help me?

My Taekwondo skills weren't any help at all! I froze. I couldn't even try to get away. I just froze. I had to wait for them to let me go. They were completely in control. Nina was the main one as always, but hidden in that little alleyway all the others found a voice too. They were saying the same things over and over again. Apparently they 'know' I'm a lezzer. They said I'm not welcome in 'their' school and that I'm disgusting.

Disgusting. Now there's something I felt before. Having it screamed in my face made sure that I felt that way again. I didn't say anything or do anything. What was I supposed to say or do? Nothing would have made a difference. I was their target for the year and they were obviously bored with just bumping in to me in the corridor.

Like every other day, I walked home, came inside, got changed and took Reggie out for his walk. But yesterday was not like any other day.

I was too scared to let Reggie off the lead. I needed him near me. He seemed to understand because for the first time in the history of our walks he didn't pull on the lead as we got to the park. He stayed right by my side. I felt safe because he was with me. I've read somewhere that animals have a sixth sense about the way their owners are feeling but I didn't believe it until yesterday. I found a bench. We sat together. I cried.

Reggie didn't try and get away, he didn't look around at what else was going on or which dogs he wanted to chase. He just sat. I didn't feel alone any more.

I thought I'd hit rock bottom over Christmas but that was nothing. After everything I been through, everything that Mum has done to give me a fresh start, all those hours that Jane has spent helping me…I have tried so hard to make it all work.

For the first time I wondered what the point was. If my life was just going to be a rollercoaster of crap then I'm not sure I wanted it any more. I thought it might just be better if I wasn't here at all.

At that moment, Reggie put his head on my knee. He looked at me and I could see that someone loved me. That made me cry more. Throughout everything he had kept me going. He'd had a crap start but it didn't stop him trusting me. I needed to trust someone. I needed to ask for help.

I called Jane. She didn't answer. I didn't think she would as she was probably still at work but I was gutted. I sat on that bench thinking about what Jane would say. She'd probably tell Mum now that they'd got more physical. She would tell me to think about what I had achieved and how nobody gets the better of me. She would tell me to do some Taekwondo and spend time with Reggie. She would tell me she loved me. She'd probably also tell me to write in my journal!

I got up from the bench and let Reggie off the lead. It wasn't fair on him not to have a run around! He didn't run anywhere and still stayed right by my side. He walked me home!

Jane has talked about making decisions before. She said that sometimes you just have to decide that you are going to carry on and you are going to succeed. Once you have made the decision, then you figure out how to make it happen. Right now, my only success will be making it through school tomorrow. I know that I really do want to be here and I know that it won't always be like this but I am terrified about what they'll do next. I know that I can't cope if this carries on and I know that if it happens again I will tell someone. It's not like life can get any worse at school! Never mind my other goals and stuff. All I want to do at the moment is get through tomorrow. Only two more days until the weekend.

# Forty

It's Friday. I did what I set out to do and got through school. I was sticking to busy places, trying to mix with the crowds so they couldn't get me even if they were planning to. I changed the routes I used to classes and spent the whole of break in the toilet. The whole thing was so frightening. Not just because of what they did to me (which was bad enough), but because of how I felt in the park. I will never, ever let anyone make me feel like that again.

Mum has been telling me since the rape that I am not a victim, and yet I have been acting like one since we got here. Maybe if I had made more effort to start with and not hidden away I would have made some friends as not been seen as a total freak. I'm not saying it's my fault, I know it isn't. It's their fault as they are choosing to behave like this. I just wonder if I could have made life a little bit easier for myself. It's never too late to make an effort I suppose.

I am not a victim.

Today at school we had an ex-pupil come and talk to us and her timing could not have been better. She went to this school and whilst she wasn't bullied she said that she didn't really have any friends. She had a few comments from other kids because she was considered different but they pretty much left her alone. She didn't go into details about her childhood but said she'd had a difficult time and lived with a local foster family while she went to school. There were always other kids coming and going so she never knew what she'd be going home to. Some of her foster brothers went to the boxing club just down the road from their house and one night she thought she'd join them. It was really unusual for a girl to do boxing but the coach helped her out and she turned out to be really good at it. She said that she was called a lesbian or a transvestite because she started to develop muscles…but nobody would really mess with her! What really annoyed people was that she would never, ever retaliate. She just smiled. She said her coach had told her to do that. She was told that the skills she had weren't supposed to be used outside of the boxing ring and she needed to be disciplined. It sounded a lot like Taekwondo except I'm still not very good at it, and the other day I couldn't have used the skills even if I'd wanted to!

I couldn't believe she just smiled at the people who were bullying her. Smiling? Like I want to smile at those girls! The only positive might be that it would annoy them, but I don't think I want to annoy them. What would they do then? I don't think I could ever beat them.

She had just come back from the World Championships with a gold medal. She had beaten everyone! She had worked really hard and she had achieved her goal. She had a really crap time growing up but it didn't stop her. More than that, it made her even more determined. That has got to be a better use of time and energy than sitting on a park bench and crying? I don't want to be a boxer, I'm not sure what I do want to be but I do know that there is more to life than being constantly frightened.

As I was leaving the room I stopped and said, 'Thank you, what you said has really inspired me.'

She just smiled and said, 'You're welcome…now whatever you have seen in me, it's already in you…go and be your own hero.' I will never forget those words.

What do I need to do to become my own hero?

I need to achieve my goals to start with. She said that she had the big goal of one day being a World Champion and then lots of smaller goals that led to it. My big Taekwondo goal is to have a black belt and so all of the other belts will lead me to the big goal. I'm not sure if I want to compete, I want to feel safe and I want to keep fit. I need to figure out what I want to do with my life so that I can have a big goal to work towards. Passing my exams feels big enough at the moment!

- It is June and I have my second belt in Taekwondo!
- It is August and I have passed all of my exams.
- It is September and I have decided what I want to do next in my life.

The successes I have had today:

- I have made it through school. I know that might sound really small but it has taken every bit of strength I have to come in to school these last two days.

The things I am grateful for today:

- Reggie! He always has to be top of the list!
- Having the talk at school today. It has really inspired me to do something with my life. I'm not completely sure what yet but I will do something.
- Talking with Jane.

I called Jane this evening and told her that things had got worse. She was obviously worried, but then I told her about today. I said that I felt much stronger and that I didn't know what I was going to do but I was going to do something! That seems to be my answer to everything at the moment. She said that she would call me on Wednesday evening and if things hadn't changed we agreed we'd talk to Mum and go to the school. I just feel so much better after today, especially knowing we have a back-up plan!

# Forty-One

I was on my way to Maths this morning, which is never a great start to the day anyway. I always see them before this lesson and there's no other way to get to the class unless I hide in the loo and make myself late. The Maths teacher isn't someone to be messed with so I have always just walked past, kept my head down and tried to ignore what they're saying. I try to make sure they can't see it's bothering me. As usual, I was walking down the corridor and I could see them ahead of me. I braced myself and right on cue I heard, 'Here comes the dyke,' come tumbling out of the Nina's mouth.

Today, I didn't keep my head down. I didn't just keep walking, looking at the floor as if it was me who should be hiding. I hadn't done anything wrong. I looked straight into Nina's eyes and with a slight smile and shake of my head, the same way Mum does when she's disappointed I haven't tidied up, I walked away.

I had beaten them. In my own small way, I had taken back the power. I didn't avoid them, hang my head in shame or try to make myself invisible. I stood tall and I did not back down. Having a corridor full of people helped a little bit as I was sure that they wouldn't try and pin me to the wall there and then!

I am proud of myself. It's the first step I have taken since the dark day sitting on a park bench wondering what the point is. It's amazing that even though I'm still feeling scared about what they might do next; I'm also feeling much stronger. If I can take that little step then I do it again and I can do whatever it takes to get through school.

In that Maths class I concentrated more than I have ever concentrated before. I felt awake and energised. I still didn't understand most of what the teacher was talking about, but I wasn't fazed by trying to work it out! I was chatting when we worked in a group and eventually got one of the questions right. It's like part of my brain had been set free. I was so scared when I looked Nina in the eye, but what did I have to lose? It couldn't get much worse and I knew that I had my back-up plan if it all went wrong!

It was the same before but I had Mum and Jane to help me figure out what I needed to do. When the police first came round after it happened I was so frightened. I didn't want to say anything, couldn't look them in the eye and just wanted to make myself invisible. I felt like I had done something wrong and no matter what anyone said, it took ages for me to stop feeling like that. When I started to actually talk to the police officers rather than just answer their questions, I felt more in control. They were answering my questions! I just needed to be braver than I was being. It seemed like an impossible task but as soon as I started asking about what would happen and what I needed to do I started to feel better. I was so worried and frightened about the unknown but also too scared to ask questions as I wasn't sure I wanted to hear the answers! Hearing the answers was always better. That way, I knew what I was dealing with!

Now, I don't really have any questions that I need the answer to. Nobody can tell me if they'll stop or whether they will continue shouting in my face until the end of the year. I can ask myself a question though! What am I going to do to make sure I get what I want out of this year? Today showed me that I can make sure I feel okay no matter what they say or do. The only thing that changed today was my reaction. Nothing they did changed at all! Yet, I felt so much better. I didn't see them again today, which was brilliant, but I noticed that I wasn't as worried about it either. I still looked around to see if they were there but my palms stayed dry. That's progress.

I know that I might have to find the energy to do the same thing every day. If that's what it takes then that is what I will do. There are lots of things I want to do that will probably mean I need to find the energy to be brave! Like, achieving these goals…!

- It is June and I have my second belt in Taekwondo!
- It is August and I have passed all of my exams.
- It is September and I have decided what I want to do next in my life.

I'm on track with these. Especially after today when it turns out all I need to do is concentrate in Maths and I might actually be okay at it!

The successes I have had today:

- I didn't walk along wishing the ground would swallow me up. I looked Nina in the eye! Mum would have been proud of my 'disappointed' look too!
- I figured out the answer to a maths question!
- I have learnt a new move in Taekwondo that will help me reach my next belt.

The things I am grateful for today:

- Reggie – especially as he is still not running too far away from me!
- All the other people in the corridor that made me feel a little bit protected!

Bring on tomorrow!

# Forty-Two

Things have been okay over the last week. I've had to make an effort to carry on just going about my day like nothing is wrong. I still look Nina in the eye as I walk past and she has actually quietened down a bit. She has plenty to say once she has walked past me but is losing the ability to say it to my face. She's not nearly as confident as she looks. When her gaggle were with her and I just looked down she had all the confidence in the world. That's not real confidence though. She has tried to avoid my eye contact a couple of times by deliberately turning to talk to one of her support crew. They were making their usual comments about me and still thought that they were hilarious, but they are not having the same effect on me at all.

I realised that while my brain has been occupied with avoiding the gaggle and being worried about what might happen I have missed out on so much. I've been writing these goals down but not doing much about the school ones. I think that Taekwondo was more of a distraction than anything and even though I was enjoying it, I wasn't 100 per cent there. Now when I go, I only think about what is going on in the room. My mind isn't wandering to the next day and how I'm going to get around school without being seen. I'm enjoying it even more and actually getting better much quicker. I'm almost back to a healthy weight too and my favourite jeans fit me again! Not only do they fit me, I wore then out to the cinema with Katie. Our mums decided that they'd like to have time to talk without having to constantly watch the dogs, so they dropped us off to have dinner and go to the cinema and they went on to somewhere a bit nicer! I really enjoyed it.

There's a big difference between how I am in school now and how I was before. I have made more effort in class and haven't just sat there like a stuffed toy feeling like I should apologise for my existence. A couple of days ago, in Science, I was working with two other girls that I haven't really spoken to before. Usually I would be really quiet and just wait for everyone else to come up with the idea but this time I had an advantage. We were doing an experiment on the effect of temperature on solubility (yawn) and I had already done this in my last school. 'Okay, so solids are usually more soluble in hot water than in cold water so we can just measure the difference in boiling water and an ice bath. We just need to measure it, draw a graph and we're done. If we use ammonium chloride it just means someone is going to have to look like an idiot and wear the safety glasses.'

A teacher's voice piped up at that moment with, 'I think you'll find, Danielle, that you'll all have to look like idiots and wear the safety glasses.' Oops! I was actually useful to my team and I had a laugh. I think that was the first time I had laughed in a lesson since I moved to this school. That's really sad isn't it?

One of the girls I was working with even asked what I was doing for lunch. I was really tempted as I was having a great time with them but that would have meant not having lunch with Katie, Maya and Callie. They had been my lifeline and I wasn't willing to change that even for one day. I am so grateful to them and I think it would be wrong of me to ditch them the first time I have another offer! It made my day to be asked though!

Things are looking up and it's only me who has changed. Even though I feel like I am making an effort, it's also really easy. The science lesson went really fast because I was having fun and I've noticed that the school days don't feel as long either. I'm definitely on target to pass my exams, but I'm not sure that's enough. I want to do well. I am more determined than ever to reach my goals.

Jane called a few days ago like she said she would and she has called every night since! We are not putting plan 'b' into action as I really am doing okay. It took me a while to convince her that I really am doing okay! She has been helping me to concentrate on the good stuff and that's making sure I don't go back to concentrating on what might happen with Nina. It was very easy to fall into a habit of only thinking about her and what she might do next. It hasn't been as easy to change that habit but I'm getting there and it's making such a big difference. Mum has noticed a change in me too. We took Reggie out together over the weekend and she told me that she'd seen me smiling much more. She said I was looking great too and said we could go shopping when she's paid! I'm never going to need the bigger sized clothes again so they're going on eBay! Maybe one day I'll tell her about what has been happening but for now, I'm just pleased that she can see that I'm okay.

Jane keeps telling me how important it is for me to do this too! I didn't tell her that I'm not doing it every day even though she probably knows that! My goals are still…

- It is June and I have my second belt in Taekwondo!
- It is August and I have passed all of my exams.
- It is September and I have decided what I want to do next in my life.

I am on target with the first two! I need to really start thinking about the last one.

The successes I have had today:

- Concentrating properly at Taekwondo and in lessons.
- Reaching my healthiest weight in almost a year.

The things I am grateful for today:

- Reggie…and no rain when I took him out for his walk – makes a change!
- Lunch with Katie, Maya and Callie.
- Laughing in class – that wasn't today, but I'm still grateful!

# Forty-Three

'Okay, Danielle, so the black belt idea is brilliant but tell me what you've done to get closer to it rather than just wishing you could do that flying kick.' Another call with Jane was turning into a motivational speech.

'I am doing stuff every day, I really am. I'm practising and learning the moves and can do the waist high kick like a pro, well almost a pro, okay so I can kick a bit! I'm getting better though, when I started I was out of breath in the warm up. School's okay and I'm feeling much more awake in class, I only think about the flying kick when I'm really bored! Don't sigh, I'm joking. I just feel like I need to get these things, I need to get my black belt and pass my exams to prove that I'm worth something.'

I should have known that would send her into another speech. 'If you're not enough without them, Danielle, then you won't be enough with them. The simple fact that you are working towards these things makes me incredibly proud and I hope you feel proud too. Don't roll your eyes, I know you're rolling your eyes.' Damn, that woman is good.

I guess everything is done taking little steps. I just want everything to happen NOW!

When we first had Reggie I wished he would learn to lie down when we told him to. That took AGES and a lot of patience from me and Mum. We had to do a little bit of training with him every day until he finally lay down on command. It's not like we don't have setbacks! I told him to sit and then lie down in the park the other day. He did it, but rather than waiting until I got to him like he usually does, he decided that chasing after a squirrel would be much more fun. So much for all those hours of training! He's good though, we just have to make sure we stick to the same rules with him and keep on, day by day, with the training. I need to do that with myself too! I don't need to lie down in a park but I do need to do something every day to make sure I get to where I want to be. Just sitting around wishing I was already a black belt isn't going to make that happen!

I'm a bit like Reggie with distractions too though. If there's something that looks more fun, even if it's just something on TV or messaging Katie, I can easily be distracted from homework. That's normal, I know that, but I don't just want to be 'normal'. I want to do well and I want to be somebody. I want to do something with my life that can make a difference. Watching TV isn't going to help me do that! I have started to do my homework as soon as I come home from walking Reggie. That way, I know that I won't be distracted and then I can watch TV as a reward later on if I've done it all. Usually, I finish my homework in half the time it would have taken me if I was just wandering around the house, watching a bit of TV and playing on my phone!

I've got a little plan up in my room now and that's keeping me on track. It's another of Jane's bright ideas! Every day I have a plan for what I'm going to do…to the finest detail! I have been sticking to it and I'm getting so much more done. I've ended up having more free time than I thought too, which can only be a good thing!

Doing something every day is something that I've done, on and off, for a while. Looking back, when I've been doing this, things have gone really well and when I haven't, things have gone a bit wrong! After I was raped, I literally went back to basics, like starting with getting up, showered and dressed. I didn't want to but doing that at the start of everyday really helped me. Then I gradually set myself little challenges, like seeing people again or leaving the house to go the shops. Gradually, day by day, things got better. If I hadn't done those things and gradually set myself more things to do, I would still be under a duvet, crying. As much as that still feels tempting occasionally, I am really pleased I made the effort and I am where I am now.

With the bullies too, it took tiny steps every day since that first eye-contact breakthrough to make me feel different. They still call me names and laugh to each other as I walk past but they're getting quieter and they haven't done anything physical since that day. I know that it could still be a million times better at school, but I took those steps and made a change. Every day, I feel a bit better about it. When I wasn't doing anything to help myself, I felt worse every day! I'm no genius but I know how I'd rather feel!

I always feel better after I've been to Taekwondo too. Even though sometimes I don't want to go if I'm tired! It's funny that after I've exercised I feel much more motivated to do other stuff too. Even homework! It means I'm doubly productive! It doesn't work the other way around though.

So, these goals that will help me concentrate on where I am now are…

- It is June and I have my second belt in Taekwondo!
- It is August and I have passed all of my exams.
- It is September and I have decided what I want to do next in my life.

The successes I have had today:

- Being super productive!
- I chose to eat yoghurt and fruit instead of chocolate! I feel great and a bit smug!
- Not being worried at school!

The things I am grateful for today:

- Reggie!
- Talking to Jane and feeling better about what I'm achieving now.

# Forty-Four

I've had such a nice day! Mum took me out for Sunday lunch and couldn't stop telling me how wonderful she thinks I am! Always a pleasure!

'I'm really proud of you, you know that don't you? Despite the fact that you're costing me a fortune in clothes, you are looking fantastic. I'll carry on making sure we have good, healthy food at home and I'm sorry that I didn't help by buying all the crisps and biscuits. I didn't want to upset you by talking about your weight, I thought I'd leave that to Jane!' What would we do without Jane?! I'd be the size of a bus and Mum wouldn't have said a thing!

'The way you're achieving so much in Taekwondo is just brilliant too. I was worried that you wouldn't stick with it but you've certainly proven me wrong. I loved watching you at your grading for your first belt. I was so proud, I still am. I was tempted to give it a go myself but I guess that would be a bit embarrassing for you?' YEP!

'With Reggie too, you haven't got bored with walking him and you have definitely become queen of the poo bags.' Wow, now there's title I always wanted. 'I did wonder if I'd be left to do the early mornings, especially through the winter. You've done so much more than I thought you would and he is such a happy dog, that's down to you and the amount of time you've invested in him.'

'So you didn't have much faith in me at all,' I joked. 'Reggie means everything to me and that I love that we adopted him! I'm so grateful that you let us have him and didn't make us have a smaller dog! I don't think I'd feel as safe walking around the park with a yapping rat on a lead!'

She agreed and said she feels safe walking him too. That really surprised me. Not that she feels safe, but that she would feel unsafe. I suppose I never really felt unsafe until I was raped and

I've been super-aware of feeling unsafe ever since. I guess most people feel vulnerable at some time or another. Especially when they've been directly involved with the crap that can happen.

Then the dreaded subject of school…! Mum was really nice about it, saying how pleased she was that I was doing well and that I'd caught up. She said I seem much happier now too! Then she said something that annoyed me a bit! She said that she was worried I wasn't making an effort with making friends! I think she could see from my face that she'd hit a nerve. I was about to start ranting that she had no idea how hard it had been, blah, blah, blah until I realised that she really didn't have a clue how hard it had been because I hadn't told her!

I told her almost everything. I missed out the bit about being called a lezzer and a dyke! I just said that they made comments and didn't go into details. Thankfully she didn't ask about what they were saying and she just sat there, stunned. She said she had no idea. She apologised for not taking more notice and asked why I hadn't told her. I said I didn't want to worry her! Apparently she was worried anyway so that master plan didn't work! I told her that Jane knew and that she'd really helped. I think Jane might be getting a phone call from Mum later, but I know Jane can work her way out of anything! I've sent her a warning text and she just said not to worry and it would be fine! Mum said that she thought I was feeling so down because I wasn't coping with what had happened. She was upset that I'd had something else to cope with on top of that. She cried and just said she was so proud of me!

I'm glad I told her and I'm really pleased that I could also tell her that I'm okay now! I realised that Mum has actually been proud of me this whole time. I thought that passing my exams and getting my belts would make her proud but she just laughed! In a good way! She said that all those things were brilliant and that she wanted me to do well, but that she was simply proud of me for being me. All that time it was my own head that was making me feel like I'm not good enough and that I need to do all these things to make other people see I'm worth something. I am worth something just as I am. Talking to Mum about it hasn't made me want to give up on these things though. I want to do well, but I want to do well for me! I want to achieve these things to prove to myself I can do it.

- It is June and I have my second belt in Taekwondo!
- It is August and I have passed all of my exams.
- It is September and I have decided what I want to do next in my life.

I'm getting there with my second belt – getting closer to that black belt! School work is on track and I know that I want to do something worthwhile. I just need to figure out what that is!

The successes I have had today:

- Figuring out that I'm actually doing okay just as I am!

The things I am grateful for today:

- Reggie…and a long walk after a massive dinner!
- The massive dinner!
- Talking to Mum.

# Forty-Five

I guess the bubble was going to burst sometime.

On the way home from school this evening I saw the headline… 'Local Girl Attacked.'

All those old familiar feels came flooding back and I ran the rest of the way home. Mum was already there when I got home. She said she had left work early as she didn't want me to be on my own if I'd seen the news. We put the TV on and the local news was reporting that a young, teenage girl had been raped. I thought I could watch it but I switched it off. It was like I was back there; they were saying the same things that they said when it was me.

Mum said that she knew the girl's mother. Not well, but they worked in the same building and sometimes had a polite chat in the queue for lunch! A friend of Mum's at work said that the girl was about 14 and went to my school and had an older sister in my year but didn't know her name. All I heard was that she was 14 years old. The same age that I was.

We got ready to take Reggie out together and I think we were both a bit nervous. There were police walking around in the park and we heard a siren in the distance. I have no idea if it was even linked to the girl being attacked but it made my heart race. Reggie was using his sixth sense again and stayed with us. We didn't see many people out, a lot less than usual and I wondered if that had happened where we used to live.

Mum said that I didn't have to go to Taekwondo if I didn't want to as people would probably be talking about it and I might not want to hear it. I hadn't even thought of that! Of course people will be talking about it. I really wasn't sure if I wanted to hear it but I also didn't really want to stay inside as I wasn't sure I'd be able to stay away from the biscuits. I know where that cycle of misery leads and I am not going there again. I was sure that I'd be okay at Taekwondo as we weren't allowed to chat while we were training anyway! Mum said she'd stay and watch so that if I wanted to come home early I could.

I think Mum had a worse evening that I did, she had to sit with some of the other parents and it was all they were talking about. She looked upset and exhausted by the time we got home. It was new to her too. When it happened to me, she was at home. Looking after me, dealing with the police and trying to keep things 'normal' for me. She wasn't with her friends so didn't know what they were saying. I think this evening was quite overwhelming for her. She didn't tell me what they were saying and I didn't ask.

In the middle of training, I did have an idea though. I get my best ideas when I'm exercising. 'I want to send them a card. I felt so much support when I read the cards that I'd been sent. I wanted to be able to do that for someone else. It's not like there's anywhere you can really go as a kid to get support and know that you're not on your own. The card would be a start though, at least she would know that there is a way through this and things really can get better.' Mum said that was a brilliant idea and if I didn't mind, she would like to do the same for the girl's Mum. She'd had a few cards from parents of children who had been raped and she said that they'd really helped her. We decided we'd keep it simple as nobody has the energy to read an essay when you feel like that! Mum said she'd get the cards tomorrow and she would ask her friend for the address. That gives me a little bit of time to figure out exactly what I am going to say!

I had been so caught up in how I was feeling hearing the news that I had forgotten about the girl who is going through hell. I felt bad about that but pleased that I can do something to hopefully make a little difference.

It seems almost selfish to think about myself when I know this has happened, but I need to focus on the good stuff. If I don't, I know what will happen and I'm not going there.

Even though it seems unimportant at the moment, here are my goals:

- It is June and I have my second belt in Taekwondo!
- It is August and I have passed all of my exams.
- It is September and I have decided what I want to do next in my life.

The successes I have had today:

- Going to Taekwondo
- I did have a good day at school but that really doesn't matter now.

The things I am grateful for today:

- Reggie! He stayed with us and kept us safe.
- Mum coming home from work early and staying to watch Taekwondo.
- Being able to send a card that will hopefully help someone else who is having the most horrible time ever. That doesn't really explain it but I have never been able to find the words!

# Forty-Six

I was quite happily up in my room and Mum said that she was going to call to get the address so we could send our cards. I was figuring out what to write in mine and had done quite a few drafts. I wonder if the people who sent me cards did the same thing?

It's hard to know what to write because, even though I've experienced it too, I don't know exactly how she is feeling. I only know how I was feeling at the time! I had decided that I probably wouldn't have wanted someone telling me how things would get better and that one day I would be happier than I ever thought possible – okay…that's an exaggeration! So, I settled on saying,

> *As hard as this is right now, take one day at a time.*
> *You are stronger than you think you are, and you are not on your own.*

I wasn't sure about whether or not to sign my full name as apparently her sister is in my year so I just signed it, 'love, Dani (a fellow survivor)' and put my email address. As I was sealing up the envelope, Mum came in.

'I've been thinking about what to write in my card,' she said. 'I can't find the words and that has made me think. How would you feel about me offering to be there if the girl's mum ever wanted to talk? I felt really alone when it happened to you. If it wasn't for Jane I don't think I would have coped. I didn't know how to help you or whether what I was doing and saying was right. I just felt completely out my depth.'

If she did that, and the Mum got in touch that would mean people would know.

Since moving here, my biggest fear has been that people would find out. Mum has said that she won't do anything until

I've decided and she's completely happy either way. She also said that maybe I could think about offering the same thing to the girl. That sounded like something I wouldn't mind doing. I would have loved someone my own age to talk to when it happened to me. It's not just that it would have been nice if someone really understood what I was going through but just having someone who didn't tread on eggshells around me would have been nice! Maybe it would be nice to do that for someone else.

What's the worst that could happen? What have I got to lose? If people at school found out then maybe they wouldn't speak to me. I've experienced that for almost a whole year so it's not something that feels that scary anymore! Maybe people wouldn't find out anyway; it's nearly the end of term so I'm guessing she won't go back to school until next year unless she really wants to. It's not like she'd be the first to tell people about me; she'll know how hard it is. I'll be the last thing on her mind!

It's not like I'll be shouting it from the rooftops. I'd just be offering to chat to her if she wants me to. Same with Mum. The chances are that they'll be so preoccupied with everything that's going on, they won't get in touch. Or, like with me, her mum might not show her the cards yet! So, it might not be the worst thing in the world. All I'm doing is offering to help someone. If people find out then I'll just have to figure out what to do next. I haven't done anything wrong so I shouldn't be frightened. I can't really be of any help to this girl if I'm still full of fear. That's not a great role model for her is it? She hasn't done anything wrong either so she shouldn't feel like she has to hide away. Maybe by me offering to help, she'll see that.

I haven't really thought about it in detail until now. I just had it in my head that I didn't want people to know. I felt that I had a dirty secret yet I hadn't done anything wrong! I kept thinking, *People will find out about me*. Well, they're not finding out about 'me'. They are just hearing about something that happened to me. That doesn't actually tell them anything about who I am. That's what this girl needs to know too. I can't believe it's taken me this long to figure it out.

I have told Mum that I'll do it too, that in her card she can offer that we'll both be there if they need anything. Maybe this is something I can do that's worthwhile. Even just knowing that she's not completely on her own might help a bit. I can do that for someone else.

I feel so much better now that I have made the decision. I think that because I've been so scared of people finding out, I've hidden lots of other things about me too. I haven't really relaxed and let people get to know me properly. I've always been on guard. I think this counts as a pretty big success for today!

My head is full of other stuff at the moment but I'm still on track with my three goals:

- It is June and I have my second belt in Taekwondo!
- It is August and I have passed all of my exams.
- It is September and I have decided what I want to do next in my life.

I might even have started to find out what I'd like to do next in my life. It feels good that I might be able to help someone who's having a horrible time.

The successes I have had today:

- Figuring out all of that stuff! Jane was right, writing helps!

- The things I am grateful for today:
- Reggie! He sat quietly, half asleep and half watching as I decided what to write in the card.
- Mum prompting me to make something positive come from what happened to me.

# Forty-Seven

Beep Beep. 'Thank you for the cards, I can't tell you how much they mean to us. If it would still be okay, I would really appreciate talking to you, Angie x.'

Mum replied straight away. 'I'm free all over the weekend so could talk anytime x.'

They started talking almost immediately and I decided I didn't want to listen so went for a long walk with Reggie. An hour and a half later, I came home and they were still on the phone!

I waved at Mum as I left for my Saturday Taekwondo session as it looked like she would be on the phone for a long, long time! I'm glad I went because I needed the distraction. I was nervous that I was no longer anonymous. I guess it's the fear of the unknown again. An hour of training was really good for me and by the time I got home I felt like I was ready to cope with anything! It was a good job as Mum said that if I was up for it, we were going over to their house! My mum really is an 'all or nothing' woman!

I panicked. Mum said that I didn't have to go and that if I did go and wanted to leave at any point, we would leave. She said her priority was me and my wellbeing over and above anyone else's! The girls name is Amie and her mum is Angie. Mum said it felt good that she was able to listen and that she could really identify with what Angie was saying. She said that Amie's sister was also struggling as she didn't know what to do or say. That was it. I knew I had to go. That was the feeling I remembered more than anything. When you just want someone to talk to you about ANYTHING! Just to talk like they always had done. It must be even worse when that person is your sister and you're used to them talking to you all the time! I wanted to go and try and just make things a little bit better for her.

I showered, changed in to my favourite jeans and over lunch asked Mum about what had happened. Mum was a bit upset as she said it was similar to what happened to me. She was on her way home from a friend's house and thought she was being followed. It was an older man who raped her and he had been caught a couple of days later. He has now been charged and is in custody. I thought about how frightened she must have been for that couple of days. He was caught because he tried to do it again, but the woman managed to get away and call the police almost immediately. That could have been so much worse. It makes my skin crawl just thinking about it. Mum said that she's not sure if Amie will want to talk for long as she's been given some pills to help her sleep, but we can just go over for a cuppa (Mum's answer to everything!) and see what happens.

The genius that I am, I didn't even ask about Amie's sister as I was so busy trying to think about what I could say that might help!

I think Mum was as nervous as I was as she knocked on the door. Angie opened the door and standing right behind her was Nina Bloody Devlin.

We walked inside and Mum just hugged Angie. That lovely moment was lost on me as I just stood in their hallway trying not to look at Nina. Angie introduced us after what seemed like a lifetime and didn't seem to notice how awkward it was. My stomach had literally excelled itself with the ache turning into a fireball of panic that rose steadily into my chest, down my arms and into my head. I am as sure as I can be that even my ears were shaking. She offered us a drink and said, through tears, that she couldn't put into words how much she appreciated us coming over. She said she knew how hard it must have been. It was hard, but if I'd known I was coming to Nina Bloody Devlin's house I would have sprinted faster than I have ever sprinted before in the opposite direction. It was way too late to start sprinting by then.

I looked at Nina. *I will not be intimidated, I will not be intimi-*

*dated*. But when I looked at her, I saw scared and tired eyes.

She looked back at me and said in a whisper, 'I don't know how to help Amie. She's my little sister and I don't know how to help her.'

I didn't want to assume that Amie would want to talk to me, so I asked Angie if she could find out. She came back downstairs saying that Amie was awake and would like me to go up. I went up and introduced myself and saw a book lying on the floor. I'd read it in my old school and I asked her if she was enjoying it. Amie smiled and said, 'No.'

'I'm not surprised, it almost bored me tears.'

That broke the ice. 'Not as bad as Maths though is it?' she said. 'I'd read that book every week if it meant I never had to look at numbers again.' She looked at me as if she was waiting for something. I know that look. Relieved that we were talking about normal stuff and waiting for the 'r' word to be brought up. I wasn't going to do that. We talked about the book, about the music posters she had on her wall and about how much we hated Maths. I didn't need to say anything about me being a survivor as I knew Angie had told her.

Amie went quiet and said, 'How did you get through this?'

I told her the truth. 'I just take every day as it comes and set myself little tiny challenges every day. It started with getting out of bed, then within a week I'd progressed to getting out of bed, washing my hair and getting dressed. I still do it now but the challenges are bigger, like doing my homework. That's pretty big! You could try telling your sister that you just want to talk about normal stuff and that's the best way she can help.' I told her what Mum told me. 'You're not a victim. I still have bad days but there's a lot more good days now! You're stronger than you think you are!'

I came home feeling absolutely exhausted. I also had a real sense of freedom. I had done something good today. What has happened with Nina has become irrelevant. I had made a difference. That feels more important than any goal right now and is one of my biggest successes so far.

# Forty-Eight

I saw Nina at school earlier today and I think she is finding out the hard way what it's like to be alienated. I could see that her friends didn't know what to say to her and that they were all looking quite awkward around her. She was probably just thinking about her sister, but maybe she'll get a tiny experience of what it's like to feel alone. There's nothing worse than feeling completely alone in a room full of people. I spent months wishing that Nina would one day find out what it felt like. That she would be alienated too. But not like this. Nobody from her gaggle has even looked in my direction, so I am grateful that she hasn't said anything about my experience to them. If she had, I am sure I'd know about it by the way they'd look at me. It probably wouldn't be with the usual sneers and giggles.

Jane called last night to find out how it was going with Amie. 'I'm really impressed with how you're coping and how you're stepping up to help someone else.' That felt good. 'Just don't forget the other important stuff too. You need to make sure you're preparing for exams, going to Taekwondo and writing in the journal. If you don't look after yourself then you won't be in a fit state to help someone else.'

I suppose she's right, but I feel a bit selfish concentrating on that stuff when I know how hard it is for Amie. It's not long until I go for my second belt and the exam countdown is getting closer too. I need to make sure that I pass or all of this has been for nothing. Then what would Amie think of me? I wouldn't be a very good role model if I turned around and told her I didn't get my belt and I'd failed my exams!

When we were over at Amie's this evening, there was a reporter from the local press talking to Angie. She was being interviewed and Amie was upstairs as she didn't want to hear what was being said. I thought that was a good decision! I came down from Amie's room to get us a drink and heard Angie say to the reporter, 'My daughter's life is ruined.' It stopped me in my tracks. What if Amie had heard that? I am sure that right now, she's convinced that her life is ruined but what if she heard her mum say that? I'm not saying that her life won't be changed by this, or that things won't be difficult…but ruined? Her life doesn't have to be ruined. That's a pretty scary message to be giving someone.

If I had heard that back when I was still wanting to stay under the duvet I'm not sure I'd ever have left my bed. What would have been the point? My life hasn't been easy, but this year that hasn't all been to do with the fact I'm a rape survivor. My life hasn't been ruined either. Changed? Yes. Ruined? No.

If the rape hadn't happened I'd still be at my old school, I'd probably still be quite naïve and worried about what to wear for parties more than anything else. I'd still be on the hockey team and I'd never have met Nina! That all sounds quite good! But…I wouldn't have Reggie, I wouldn't have started Taekwondo, I wouldn't have met Katie, Maya and Callie, and I wouldn't have been able to help Amie. I still would delete that day from my life if I could, but not everything that has happened since has been bad. Amie needs to know that this doesn't mean her whole life is ruined.

Like Jane said, I still need to focus on the things I want to do. If I don't work on these things then I'm ruining my own chances:

- It is June and I have my second belt in Taekwondo!
- It is August and I have passed all of my exams.
- It is September and I have decided what I want to do next in my life.

The successes I have had today:

- Helping Amie.

The things I am grateful for today:

- Reggie! Even though he did run off and end up in the lake during our walk today! He's obsessed with chasing Canadian Geese!
- Laughing at Reggie swimming around the lake! I needed a laugh.
- Realising that my life really hasn't been ruined.

I'm surprised that I'm not more affected by talking with Amie about stuff. I thought it might bring back loads of old feelings and memories. In a way, I think she's helping me too. It feels good to be doing something good for someone else!

# Forty-Nine

I got my second belt in Taekwondo.

I'm so pleased and now can't wait to start working on the next one.

Every time I learn something new and especially when I pass my grading to get the belt I know I'm getting closer and closer to getting the black belt. I was really nervous before I left the house and felt like I hadn't done enough. I've been concentrating on getting ready for the exams and spending a bit of time with Amie, so I was worried that I hadn't put enough effort into training. I think that carrying on with training has helped with everything else though. Having that little bit of time just to think about something I want to do and work hard physically at the same time always makes me feel much better. It paid off yesterday and it was the best feeling ever to be told I had passed and to be presented with my new belt. I'd worked for it and I'd achieved something. That feels much better than just sitting in front of the TV and feeling sorry for myself like I was doing.

I think that if I wasn't doing Taekwondo I'd be finding it difficult to help Amie. Sometimes when I talk with her it does bring back memories and feelings that I've worked hard to move on from. If I just came home and didn't have anything else to concentrate on I think I'd be turning to the biscuits again. I have been tempted to miss training and just sit at home, but that's when it's even more important that I make the effort to get up and leave the house. It would be so easy to give up completely, but I'd be the only one losing out! That doesn't sound like the best idea I've ever had!

Mum is still seeing Angie too. I think she's feeling the same as me. She is pleased that she can try and offer a little bit of help but at the same time it's hard when it brings back all the memories. We were talking the other day about the little happy triggers we had. I still have mine and they still make me smile. We told Amie and Angie about them too and I realised that nobody was really talking to Nina. When we go over to their house, Nina usually stays in her room. I don't mind that at all, but I guess it's a pretty lonely time for her. I said to Amie that she could tell her sister about the happy triggers as it might help her too. Before I knew it, Amie had called Nina into the room with us and started telling her all about it. I had a horrible feeling that Nina would start laughing at the idea or would make a fool of me like she did at school. The fear started to rise in me and I was dreading Nina's reaction. Nina just left the room and returned a couple of minutes later carrying a wooden box about the size of a shoebox. She said that she already had happy triggers and said we could look inside. Amie opened it carefully and found pictures of her and Nina. There was the first picture of them together soon after Amie had been born right though to a photo that had been taken just days before Amie was attacked. There were little pictures that Amie had drawn as a young child and a bracelet that she had made for Nina years ago.

Nina said that her memory box was something she looked at to remember the good times and she knew that there would be good times again. I couldn't believe someone who had been such a bitch could be so lovely! I did my best not to look shocked and agreed with her that there would definitely be good times again. It was nice to be able to say that and really believe it.

I was telling Jane about what happened and said that I really didn't mind that people knew about what happened to me now. It had gone from being my biggest fear to something that really didn't matter. I was pleased I could help someone else and that felt more important. Jane asked me how I could carry on feeling like that as she said there are hundreds more Amies out there who would love to know that things really can get better. She said it's not just about Amie either but there are loads of people being bullied, moving house and having so many other things to deal with that it might feel good to help them too. I laughed saying that I don't have any more time in the day to talk to more people! She asked me what I could do to help them and I jokingly said I could write a book. Jane didn't think it was a joke and thought it was a great idea. How crazy is that? I'm just a kid! I can't write an essay without getting bored so I can't write a book!

This is what I am going to do though! I've reached the goal to get my second belt ahead of schedule so it's time for number three!

- It is September and I have my third belt in Taekwondo!
- It is August and I have passed all of my exams.
- It is September and I have decided what I want to do next in my life.

The successes I have had today:

- Getting my second belt! Okay, it was yesterday but it still counts!
- Helping Amie.

The things I am grateful for today:

- Reggie! He is lying here snoring while I write this!
- Talking to Jane.
- I'm grateful that I have met Amie as she's helping me too.

# Fifty

I spent yesterday revising but I can't really remember anything I read about. I was just reading and then worrying about the exams. That meant that nothing was really sticking in my brain. I couldn't decide what to revise so was reading bits of everything in the hope that something would stick. I can't keep doing that as it's never going to work and I really want to do well. I need a plan. That's how we do it in Taekwondo. We have little things to learn each time, we keep going over it until we know it inside out and then when we put it all together it looks brilliant. That's what I need to do here. I need to make sure I'm concentrating on a little bit at a time and I need to make sure it is all in my head in time for the exam.

I have spent the last two hours drawing out a complete plan of how I am going to revise for each exam, fit in training, walk Reggie and see Amie. I also have a study day booked with Katie, Maya and Callie, but I'm not sure we'll actually get much work done.

The plan is brilliant. It's on a massive piece of paper, its colour coded and all the exams are written in too. I've planned out my revision in order of the exams that are coming up and I'm never studying for more than 45 minutes without a break as I know I'd go insane if I tried that. I've actually got more time than I thought and that includes doing all the other things I want to do. I just need to stop thinking of study leave as 'free' time!

I put the most important things into the plan first – walking Reggie and Taekwondo. Then I put the exams in as they can't be moved. It didn't look quite as bad when I actually wrote them on the plan as I could see how spaced out they were and that I had days free in-between them. When I was just looking at them on the list the school had printed out for me it looked really scary! So, I filled in the subjects I was going to revise each day to fit in with the exams and put my break times in too. I still had time to see Amie and to chill out in the evenings with Mum on the nights I'm not going to Taekwondo. It was quite easy to sort out what I needed to do and when I needed to do it when I just sat down and drew it out. It looks good too as Reggie and Taekwondo have their own colours and then each exam is colour coded with the revision sessions in the same colour! Maybe I should have taken art instead of PE?!

I actually do think that it has been a good use of time even though I probably could have been revising in those two hours! If I stick to the plan then I know that I can walk into every exam feeling prepared. All I need to do now is actually stick to the plan! I'll add it to the list of goals!

I'm not seeing Amie today and it's quite nice to have a day just to focus on my own stuff. I keep getting the comment about writing a book popping into my head too! It would be so cool to see a book that I'd written on the shelf in a bookshop, but I have no idea how I could do that! How would I even start and what would I write?! I'd love to be able to help loads of people but I still think its way out of my league!

According to my plan for the day it's nearly lunchtime so I can definitely stick to that! Then I can get stuck in to some exciting Geography revision! It seems so much easier knowing that I only have to do 45 minutes at a time and I know exactly what I'm looking at in that time! I wouldn't say I'm looking forward to it as who would get excited about plate tectonics but very soon I will never have to think about geography again!

I have an extra goal now for the next few weeks:

- I have finished my last exam and I have stuck to my plan every day.
- It is September and I have my third belt in Taekwondo!
- It is August and I have passed all of my exams.
- It is September and I have decided what I want to do next

in my life.

The successes I have had today:

- Coming up with a genius plan to get my revision done and fit in everything else too.
- Not putting the TV on even though I have been tempted!

The things I am grateful for today:

- Reggie!
- Having a whole day just to do my own stuff.
- Mum leaving me a really nice lunch ready!

# Fifty-One

Today was the first day of exams.

Two in one day.

Geography first and then RE, that was never going to be fun, was it?! Mum said she'd take Reggie this morning so I could have more time but I didn't want her to. Going out with Reggie is the best way to start the day. When we got home she had prepared an energy filled breakfast to help me through the morning, and a packed lunch that would apparently keep me full of energy all through the afternoon! If only they also contained the questions and the answers.

When the doors opened to the exam hall, everyone went quiet and then filed in. We were told where to sit and before I could find my favourite pen the exam paper was dropped onto my desk and the clock had started ticking. Literally. It was really annoying! Geography went okay I think. It wasn't that hard and luckily I had revised almost all of the topics that came up. I had a go at answering all of the questions and felt quite pleased with myself as I had finished about two minutes before we were told to put our pens down. I walked out of the exam hall hoping that all the exams would be like that!

'Mum, that NRG brekki worked. My tum didn't rumble. Yay! X.'

I settled down in the corner of the sports field to eat my lunch and read through my RE revision notes. I wasn't feeling that nervous as I'd stuck to my plan and all I really did in RE was listen to other people rant on about their opinions and argue over what they thought was right and wrong! The best thing about RE was that our teacher would sometimes use motivational videos, usually about sport, to show how people could overcome barriers in their lives. I loved those! Not sure they'll help me right now though!

I was back in the exam hall and this time had my favourite pen in hand. I still use the red ones that Jane gave me when I was told I couldn't wear my bracelet. Nobody had noticed that I'd been wearing it since Christmas. The first question was nice and easy about Christianity and the Sacraments. I had revised that and I felt like I was on a roll! I turned the page and there was a question I had not prepared for.

'Abortion is right in certain circumstances'.

i. Do you agree? Give reasons for your opinion.
ii. Give reasons why some people may disagree with you.

I remembered that lesson; everyone giving their opinions and talking about the reasons why a woman might choose to have an abortion. They were talking about rape as the obvious reason why a woman might choose to have an abortion. I then had to sit and write about it in an exam.

I took a deep breath and looked around. Most people were scribbling away. It was just another question to them, just another opinion that they would try and make sound smart to pick up extra marks. Nobody could see how hard this as for me. As I looked up, I realised that I might not be the only one finding this hard. Nina was taking this exam too. There could be other people who were struggling. I had no idea.

I had the bracelet on that Jane gave me, my happy trigger. I looked at the letter 'B' and remembered that Jane believed in me. All I had to do was answer the question and move on to the next one. I asked myself, *If I was Callie or Maya, what would I think?* I started writing the answer as if I was one of them. There wasn't anything personal about it at all. As soon as I started doing that I could think of lots of other reasons why a woman might choose to have an abortion and all the reasons why some people might disagree. Once I started writing it was easier to just get it over and done with and move on to the next question.

I was so relieved when I turned the page and there was a picture of The Star of David! I had revised that and happily started a brain dump on everything I knew about Judaism! I could not get out of that exam hall quickly enough once it had finished. I saw Nina as I was leaving and she asked me if I was okay! I was more shocked than anything and I was also shocked that when I said 'yes', it was the truth. I really was okay.

Part of me feels like I shouldn't feel okay if that makes sense! If I sit and think about it for long enough I could make myself feel really crap but I'm okay, I did the best I could and I'm about to get ready for Taekwondo!

This is why I'm working so hard…so I can achieve something!

My goals:

- I have finished my last exam and I have stuck to my plan every day.
- It is September and I have my third belt in Taekwondo!
- It is August and I have passed all of my exams.
- It is September and I have decided what I want to do next in my life.

The successes I have had today:

- Geography exam going well.
- Not freaking out and being affected by the question in the RE exam.

The things I am grateful for today:

- Reggie! Starting the day with him and the sun was shining.
- My breakfast and lunch!
- Nina asking if I was okay.
- Being okay!

# Fifty-Two

Mum had a call from Angie this morning saying that Amie had been rushed into hospital this morning because she tried to kill herself. I thought she was doing okay. Obviously not.

Mum didn't want to tell me because of the exams and she was worried that it might really upset me. And it has. Luckily she's recovering and Mum told me once she knew that Amie would be okay. Part of me doesn't blame Amie. I know how awful it is to start with when you really don't know how you're going to get through it. I wouldn't blame anyone for wondering if it was worth it. I often thought that it might be easier if I just wasn't around anymore. I have thought that since being here too thanks to Nina and her gang. I still wish none of it had happened but I am so glad I am here and there is so much going on in my life that I wouldn't ever want to change.

I know that Amie won't be able to see that yet. I wish I knew what to say to make a difference. I wish I could do something to show her that it really will be okay if she stays strong. Looking back though, I'm not sure I would have believed it. I had to figure it out for myself. I had a lot of help from Jane and from Mum but something in my own head had to want it to get better. It wasn't going to get better just because other people said it would. Maybe that's what I should write in a book! It would be a very short book!

It's horrible to think of Amie in hospital. At least she's safe there and she can get help. Mum said that we can go and see her tomorrow. I'm not really in the mood to write any more but thinking about Amie has made me want to try and help people more. Maybe that's linked to my goal of figuring out what I want to do with my life!

I have finished my last exam and I have stuck to my plan every day.

- It is September and I have my third belt in Taekwondo!
- It is August and I have passed all of my exams.
- It is September and I have decided what I want to do next in my life.

The successes I have had today:

- Doing some revision even though it's the last thing I want to do.

The things I am grateful for today:

- That Amie is going to be okay.

# Fifty-Three

'My life is over,' Amie said as she fought back tears. 'Totally destroyed.'

'That's not true,' I said, reaching out to take her hand in my mind.

I was trying to explain to her that she had support, she had a loving family and that as hard as it was right now, she could get through it. Nothing I said made any difference. She said that she was sorry but she wasn't as strong as me.

That was rubbish.

We're both just human beings who have had something horrible happen to us. She is strong enough to figure this out, but I don't know how to get her to see that. She just kept saying that she couldn't deal with it. As we were about to leave she said that she was even too scared to leave the house. I remembered that feeling. I was terrified at the thought of leaving the house. I hadn't felt that in a while. I asked her how she'd feel about coming out with me and Reggie! I had showed her pictures of him but she hadn't met him before. I promised her that she would feel safe with Reggie! I knew that she liked dogs because she had talked about them before. Mum and Angie had overheard and said that they'd come too. We'd all be together. Amie didn't look completely convinced but agreed to come. I don't think Angie is going to let Amie out of her sight for ages, but I don't blame her! We agreed that we'd bring Reggie over and pick them up on Saturday morning. Mum suggested that we go to a nice big Country Park about an hour away so we can have lunch and get away from the local area. I am looking forward to introducing Amie to Reggie. He's made me feel safe again so I hope he can help her too. Now, I need to revise though or I'll never achieve these goals!

- I have finished my last exam and I have stuck to my plan every day.
- It is September and I have my third belt in Taekwondo!
- It is August and I have passed all of my exams.
- It is September and I have decided what I want to do next in my life.

If I wasn't writing these down I probably wouldn't be this focused!

The successes I have had today:

- Getting Amie to agree to leave the house!

The things I am grateful for today:

- Reggie…I know he'll help Amie feel safe.
- Amie being okay…she has another chance now.
- I'm grateful that I no longer feel like there's no point.

# Fifty-Four

Yesterday's exam went well thankfully! I concentrated and wasn't too distracted. It was a PE exam so it's not like it took too much brainpower! I actually quite liked one of the questions as it was about intrinsic motivation. I know a lot about that now! Using your own feelings to motivate yourself isn't always the easiest thing in the world to do but it feels bloody good when you do it.

Getting everything out of my head and into this journal has really helped too. I was telling Amie about it this morning. She couldn't believe how much I write and that I still write down my goals and stuff!

We were out for ages today. We picked Amie and Angie up at about ten this morning. Nina was staying at home to revise and even though she's polite to me now, I was still relieved that she wasn't coming. We introduced Reggie to them both so that he wouldn't bark as they got into 'his' car and Amie fell in love with him straight away. Angie laughed and said she could understand why we felt safe with him around! She was also very quick to tell Amie that she couldn't have a dog! It was a really good day to be out as the sun was shining and the park wasn't too busy. That was a bonus as we could let Reggie off the lead to run around.

I could see that Amie was nervous to begin with. She kept looking around and checking behind her. It didn't take long for her to relax though and soon she was running after Reggie's ball so she could throw it for him. She was laughing which made Mum and Angie stop in their tracks. Angie was holding back tears but trying not to let Amie see it. We sat outside with Reggie, had our lunch and it was really good fun. Nobody was talking about what had happened or about the hospital. We were just having a day out! We were mainly talking about Reggie and laughing about how embarrassing he can be. Amie thought that

Reggie had completely fallen in love with her and was a bit disappointed when she found he'd actually fallen in love with the ham sandwich she was eating! As soon as she'd finished eating he moved over to where Angie was sitting! Lunch lasted for ages and it was really nice to just forget about everything and have fun. I'm not sure that it would have been that easy to do if Reggie wasn't there! He is such a great distraction and he always makes people happy. Well, most people!

After lunch we carried on walking around the park. Amie and I were ahead of Mum and Angie as we were throwing the ball for Reggie. I accidently threw it in the direction of another dog so Reggie went running off to say 'hello' like he does. We quickly followed and by the time we got there Reggie was licking the other dog's face! He does that quite a lot too! The owner of the other dog was a young guy and obviously wasn't happy that Reggie had come over! As I was about to apologise and call Reggie back, Amie laughed and said, 'Look, they're kissing!'

The guy snapped straight back and said, 'Don't be disgusting, they're both boys…that's so gay.'

Amy just snapped back, 'So what's wrong with that?'

I didn't even notice that the guy had walked away. I was staring at Amie in awe. She looked at me like I had gone nuts and asked me what I was staring at! I told her that I'd been called names at school and had never had the guts to stand up to them. I said that it had stopped now and obviously I didn't tell her that her sister was the ringleader! I told her that I was so impressed that she had just stood up to someone and hadn't been afraid to do it.

She said that she hated it when someone said or did something that wasn't fair, and said that she doesn't care what that guy thinks of her because what he said was wrong. She then said that she was surprised I didn't stand up to the bullies because I was the bravest person she knew.

Me? Brave? I don't feel brave!

I remembered what that ex-pupil said to me a while ago. I looked at Amie and told her that if she could see bravery in me it was only because it was in her too. She had just proven it!

I could see that she was thinking about what I'd said. I know that she has a long way to go before she's feeling properly happy again but I really think that today has made a difference to her. I know that Reggie has made a difference and it's because of Reggie that she's proven to herself how brave she can be. It feels amazing to be a part of that.

I wish that I had Amie's courage. If I'd been on my own and that guy had said that about Reggie, I probably would just have apologised and tried to get Reggie away from his dog as soon as possible. She's right though...who cares what people think? Especially when they're wrong!

I told Amie that Jane had said writing a book would be a good idea! Amie said it would be amazing and she'd read it! I said to Amie that when she's feeling ready, we could write one together. It's a deal! We might make our millions and help other people at the same time!

I need to add writing the book to my list of goals!

- I have finished my last exam and I have stuck to my plan every day.
- It is September and I have my third belt in Taekwondo!
- It is August and I have passed all of my exams.
- It is September and I have decided what I want to do next in my life.
- When Amie is ready we will write a book to help other survivors.

The successes I have had today:

- Being able to show Amie how brave she is.

The things I am grateful for today:

- Reggie! He has made a massive difference in making today a success.
- Amie and Angie coming with us!
- Learning from Amie that I need to be brave too.

# Fifty-Five

I had my last two exams today.

Finally.

I stuck to my plan and apart from the near miss in the RE exam, everything has gone well. I can't believe it's all over. I only have to go back to that place to get my results (not thinking about that yet!) and then I never have to go there again. The thing is, I'm not so bothered now and the thought of going back doesn't scare me. I'm definitely ready for the next steps though, whatever they might be!

The best thing about today was that I went out to celebrate with Katie, Maya and Callie. We had been talking about it for ages, saying that we'd meet in town and go for pizza after the last exam. I thought the day would never come!

I raced home after that final paper was collected. I could not get out of that exam hall fast enough. I had an amazing sense of relief more than anything. I wasn't worrying about whether I had done okay or what I could have done better, I was just so excited it was all finished. No more revision and no more 45 minute blocks of trying to concentrate. I am happy to say that I have done my best! Whatever happens now, I don't have any regrets and that feels great.

I got home and Jane called; I swear she has a sixth sense! Congratulations on finishing the exams. What are you doing later?' She seemed more excited than me that I was going out and celebrating. She's coming to stay soon and I can't wait to see her. Being able to show her that I really am okay and that everything that has happened this year has turned out okay is amazing. I know that she's been really worried about me and to be able to say honestly that I'm happy will hopefully mean she worries a lot less! That goes for Mum too! Jane gets a double dose of worry because she talks to me and then gets Mum calling her to talk about me too! She really does put up with a lot! She asked if I'd thought any more about what I want to do next…I know that I want to be like Jane! I want to help people and really understand the best way that I can help people. I told her that I wanted to be a psychologist like her! She told me that I could go one better and be a psychologist like ME! She said that I would be brilliant and that made me feel incredible…Dr Danielle has a nice ring to it! I am going to spend some time figuring out what I need to do next so that I can become a psychologist. More importantly today though, I am going to celebrate!

I asked the girls if they wanted to join me to take Reggie out before we met up for pizza. They said they'd rather spend time getting ready! There was a little part of me that liked the idea of going to get ready with them, but when I saw Reggie waiting for me I knew I'd made the right decision! He was very excited to see me and we had a great time in the park. I would still like them to meet Reggie. They have all been a complete lifeline throughout this year for me and none of them really know how important they have been to me. Between Reggie and the girls, they have saved me this year. I am so grateful and don't know what I would have done without them.

I'd burned off more than enough energy chasing Reggie to make sure I could enjoy my pizza! Having some time with him was like a little celebration, but every day is a celebration to Reggie! I need to be more like him and see everything as an adventure! I got ready in a couple of minutes; jeans and my favourite T-shirt. I wasn't sure why the girls needed hours to get ready and even though I'd walked home, got changed, taken Reggie out, got ready to go out and walked into town…I was still there before them! Apparently they had some sort of hair drama! I didn't really understand!

Sitting there, having pizza, I realised how lucky I am.

Not just because of the pizza. I have got everything I wanted. I am 'normal' again. I was just like any other kid who had finished their exams. We talked about all sorts of stuff, laughed a lot and got funny looks from other people when Callie got a little bit over excited by the ice cream machine. I suppose 'normal' is still a bit of a rubbish word as I don't want to just be 'normal'; I want more than that! Today was amazing though as it proved to me that things really do get better.

I need to make sure that they keep getting better! It's time to add some goals, especially as I have completed two today! They're both going on the success list! The big goal is now going to be about becoming a psychologist.

- It is September and I have my third belt in Taekwondo!
- It is August and I have passed all of my exams.
- When Amie is ready we will write a book to help other survivors.
- I am graduating with a Psychology degree and then a PhD!

I've done everything I can to make sure goal number two happens!

The successes I have had today:

- Completing two goals! I finished my exams and I did, pretty much, stick to the plan! I have also decided what I want to do with my life and now I can have fun figuring out how I am going to make that happen!

The things I am grateful for today:

- Reggie being as excited as me that I finished my exams!
- Finishing my exams.
- Talking to Jane.
- Dinner with the girls.
- A whole summer to look forward to.

# Fifty-Six

It's the first day of the summer holidays and now all I can think about is starting sixth form! When we were doing the applications I just applied for anything as I couldn't really see the point. Now, I can see that there was always a part of me that knew where I wanted to be in a few years' time. As long as I don't fail completely I will be able to go to sixth form and that will be the next step to me becoming a psychologist. Mum has called the college and asked if I can swap Geography for Psychology which thankfully they said I could! Geography? What was I thinking?! I was really pleased she called though as not only do I now get to do the right A levels but she is taking my goal seriously. She was excited for me and has no doubt I can do it!

I'm nervous about getting the results but deep down I know that I have done my best and whatever happens, I'm going to sixth form. Out of everything that I have achieved this year, the exams are only one tiny part of the story.

I survived school for a start! This morning, I started getting a similar feeling to last year… Nerves about starting somewhere new again! It is scary but it's normal to feel a bit nervous. Katie is going to be at the same sixth form which is brilliant so I already have a friend. Maya and Callie are going to an art college, which sounds like hell on earth to me but they are very excited! I am sure that we'll all still meet up though. Nina is going to this sixth form too! Six months ago that would have probably meant I was going to change my plans and go somewhere else. Now, I couldn't care less and am almost pleased that she's going to be there, so I know that she can see me succeed! I don't mean that in a bitchy way but the best form of revenge is doing really, really well! It will also be a chance for Amie to see that life gets better and that matters more to me than anything! Since spending more and more time with Reggie, Amie has decided she wants to be a vet! She laughed saying that in a few years' time we'd both be doctors and authors which sounds pretty cool. That does sound really cool! So, I'm actually excited about sixth form. I don't have any fear of people 'finding out' about my story either. I was worried that people would only see me as a victim if they knew. That hasn't happened at all. Nobody is treating me any differently because I'm not behaving differently! When I moved to this school I felt like a victim and acted like a victim. That's how I let people treat me and I became more and more of a victim. It hasn't been easy…for most of the year it's been the complete opposite of easy. But I am not a victim anymore! I don't feel like a victim or act like a victim and I'm definitely not treated like one.

I am getting closer to my third belt in Taekwondo and having the whole summer to work on it means that I might be able to go for my grading before September. I'm getting closer and closer to that black belt! I'll have the black belt before I'm a psychologist! Training hard means that I'm looking and feeling great again. I have got rid of all my big clothes and won't ever be letting myself get that unhappy again. No more turning to the biscuit tin to cheer me up!

Now I can concentrate on the goals over the summer and also enjoy myself!

- It is September and I have my third belt in Taekwondo!
- It is August and I have passed all of my exams.
- When Amie is ready we will write a book to help other survivors.
- I am graduating with a Psychology degree and then a PhD!

The success I have had today:

- Training in the living room for two hours and I finally got the move right!

The thing I am most grateful for today is knowing that what Mum wrote at the front of this journal is true. What doesn't kill you really does make you stronger.

Lodestone Books is a new imprint, which offers a broad spectrum of subjects in YA/NA literature. Compelling reading, the Teen/Young/New Adult reader is sure to find something edgy, enticing and innovative. From dystopian societies, through a whole range of fantasy, horror, science fiction and paranormal fiction, all the way to the other end of the sphere, historical drama, steam-punk adventure, and everything in between. You'll find stories of crime, coming of age and contemporary romance. Whatever your preference you will discover it here.